MANDY MORTON began her professional life as a musician. More recently, she has worked as a freelance arts journalist for national and local radio. She currently presents the radio arts magazine *The Eclectic Light Show* and lives with her partner, who is also a crime writer, in Cambridge and Cornwall, where there is always a place for an ageing long haired tabby cat.

@icloudmandy
@hettiebagshot
HettieBagshotMysteries

By Mandy Morton

The No. 2 Feline Detective Agency
Cat Among the Pumpkins

Cat Among the Pumpkins

MANDY MORTON

Allison & Busby Limited
12 Fitzroy Mews
London W1T 6DW
allisonandbusby.com

First published in 2014.
This paperback edition published by Allison & Busby in 2015.

A CIP catalogue record for this book is available from
the British Library.

10 9 8 7 6 5 4 3 2 1

ISBN 978-0-7490-1995-2

Typeset in 11.5/16.5 pt Sabon by
Allison & Busby Ltd.

The paper used for this Allison & Busby publication
has been produced from trees that have been legally sourced
from well-managed and credibly certified forests.

Printed and bound by
CPI Group (UK) Ltd, Croydon, CR0 4YY

In memory of Bruiser, a very fine outdoor cat

CHAPTER ONE

The No. 2 Feline Detective Agency had closed early so that Hettie and Tilly could prepare for their spooky night in – although no one would have noticed, as their business premises were tucked away in the back room of Betty and Beryl Butter's high street pie and pastry shop. The room had become a sanctuary, first for Hettie after her shed with a bed was taken in a storm, and then for Tilly, an arthritic tabby whom Hettie had befriended and who had fallen on hard times. The two had set up a comfortable home together, and thanks to Hettie's eye for an opportunity, they now ran a moderately successful detective agency, more by luck than judgement.

The room came cheap and the tenancy included a daily luncheon voucher to be spent in the Butters' shop, as much coal as their small fire could consume, and a garden shed for the storage of Hettie's other lives. Of those there had been many, including an almost triumphant music career which had dissolved in a haze of catnip more years ago than she cared to remember. In fact, Hettie's lives had been dominated by words like 'almost', 'nearly' and 'moderate', and the way she kept reinventing herself had only to be admired.

Of the two cats, Tilly was definitely the homemaker, with an eye for comfort and an unshakable loyalty towards Hettie and her needs. In spite of her advanced years, she had begun their friendship as Hettie's office junior and had spent many months making tea, laying fires and dusting, while Hettie sat and thought about what their office might be for and how they might make ends meet. Even in the early days, Tilly had performed the daily ritual of transforming their cosy bed sitter into a place of work. Every morning, the cloth from the table was folded away in the drawer to reveal Hettie's desk, where the business of the day was conducted; sometimes, the business of the day consisted solely of getting the cloth out again at lunchtime for the midday meal, then returning it to drawer status ready to retrieve at dinner time.

The idea of running a detective agency stemmed

from Tilly's voracious appetite for murder mysteries, which she seemed to untangle long before the various authors had finished laying down their clues. Hettie had listened with growing interest to Tilly's critique of the incompetent detectives who bumbled their way through one investigation after another, and decided that they would venture into the seamy world of the gum shoe. Her latest scheme showed very promising signs of floundering before the newly printed business cards had been distributed, and had it not been for the high-profile Furcross case – which Hettie had solved by mistake – life would have been very different.

The cats now busied themselves in preparation for their Halloween supper and scary film night. Tilly had spent the afternoon excavating two large pumpkins, while Hettie put the finishing touches to a talk she had been invited to give to the local Methodist group on how to keep their valuables safe. It had proved an impossible task, as all she could come up with was the suggestion of deep pockets or padlocks, but she knew that all they really wanted to hear about was the famous Furcross case and her heroic role in bringing justice to the small town.

'That's it. I've had enough for one day,' she said, burying her notepad under a cushion. 'What's for supper? I'm starving.'

Tilly's reply came from inside one of the pumpkins as she launched a final pawful of pale orange flesh over the side and into a bucket. 'I've ordered Beryl's Halloween pie. It's topped with a witch's hat made of pastry and comes with an extra jug of gravy. Then we're having Betty's ghost and warlock tarts for afters, and I've got a huge bag of Malkin and Sprinkle's toffee popcorn to eat later with the video.'

Hettie purred with satisfaction at the prospect of such a feast and helped her friend out of the pumpkin. 'I think you'd better clean yourself up. You look like you've just hatched from a sticky monster's egg. I'll get rid of all this gooey stuff and go round to the shop to fetch the pie.' She dragged the bucket of pumpkin flesh out into the backyard, leaving Tilly to immerse herself in the sink.

The daylight had disappeared, replaced now by a thickening icy fog which descended on cue to make the town's Halloween a night to remember. Kittens were dressed in ghoulish sheets and witches' cloaks, ready to be trotted out for tricks or treats, and as Hettie made her way round to the welcoming lights of the Butters' shop, the air was fast filling with the smoke of sitting room fires. The townsfolk settled in front of their hearths, comfortably oblivious to the fact that by the time daylight came one of them would be dead – and Hettie and her official sidekick would be bucketed into a case that the town had thought solved many years before.

The Butters' shop was filled with excited, chattering

kittens, all parading their Halloween outfits. A sea of orange and black cloaks, punctuated by the occasional white sheet, swirled this way and that as Betty handed out miniature pumpkin cakes and toffee broomsticks. Her sister Beryl manned the pie end of the shop, and mothers queued for the sought-after savouries that would grace their Halloween supper tables once the young witches and warlocks were safely tucked up in their beds.

Hettie joined the grown-ups' queue, not entirely taken with the traditional art of begging that had sprung up in the town over the last few years. To her, Halloween seemed the perfect excuse to turn offspring loose on the neighbourhood, threatening tricks to extort sweets or money, whilst parents stood at gates to collect the bounty brought triumphantly back by gangs of marauding infants. No doubt the town's economy would be boosted by the yards of orange material, black felt and tins of sweets that were sold over the counter, but it irritated Hettie to have to queue for her dinner on a cold foggy night when the only rational place to be was by a fireside.

'What a bloody nightmare!' she said as she fell over the doorstep, laden down with a giant pie, a bag of themed tarts and a jug of gravy balanced precariously on top. Tilly snatched the jug just in time, allowing Hettie to bring the pie to a crash landing on the table. 'Why we have to put up with all this nonsense every year, I'll never understand. They'll be back on the streets for Guy Fawkes Night next week. More begging, fireworks going off everywhere as soon as they get their sticky little paws on them, and no thought for those of us who can't stand the sight of kittens. They're the scourge of society as we know it, and they should all be drowned at birth.'

Tilly giggled. She was more than used to Hettie's tirades and recognised that the origins of this particular outburst lay in its being half an hour past their usual dinner time. 'Let's have the pie while it's still warm,' she said diplomatically, cutting into the pastry to release a jet of delicious-smelling vapour which seemed to calm the angry flow of infant abuse. The friends divided the pie onto plates and took two large napkins as protection from stray gravy, then settled contentedly to what Hettie liked to call 'the best bit of the day'.

It was some time before the enthusiastic licking and chewing was replaced by conversation. Satisfied at last, Hettie sat back to take in their room, marvelling at the candle-lit pumpkins in the grate and the orange and black paper chains that Tilly had hung from the picture rails. She had spent a couple of hours licking and sticking the chains that morning, and had acquired a taste for the gum on the paper – so much so that a number of the strips had lost their stickiness altogether and had been discarded in the coal scuttle.

'You've done us up a treat,' Hettie said in a rare

moment of praise, hauling herself onto her fireside armchair and settling to a leisurely cleaning of ears, paws and whiskers. 'What have you chosen for our scary movie? You were ages in the library van. I was beginning to think that Turner Page had press-ganged you into joining one of his reading groups.'

'Actually, he was doing one of those storytelling sessions where he dresses up and bangs a tambourine every so often. He was surrounded by kittens and I couldn't get to the videos until the end, so I sat and listened instead. It frightened me a bit because it was a true story.'

'Well, it can't have been any worse than the stuff you usually read,' said Hettie, glancing at the pile of library books on the edge of Tilly's blanket. Every one of them boasted the word 'murder' in the title.

'No, but this was different. He was telling the story of Milky Myers.'

'Milky Myers! I haven't heard that name for years. But it's not really true – it's just a spooky legend made up to stop kittens hanging round the old Peggledrip house.'

'Ah, but it's back in the news again. Marmite Sprat has included the story in her latest collection of *Strange But Trues*. Look – Turner Page gave me one to read.'

Hettie reached over and took the slim volume, one of many penned by the town's local and completely self-appointed historian, whose 'little books' seemed to dominate any gathering where a sale could be made. The lurid cover and cheap paper added to the charm of a gazetteer bursting with incorrect facts and finished off with the author's untrained pen and ink drawings, and she opened the book at the contents page, noting that there were four *Strange But Trues* to be had. The subjects had all been well thought out to capture the Halloween market.

'Just listen to this,' she said, holding the book to the fire for more light. '"The Headless Cat of Sheba Gardens", "Miss Pilchard's Magic Letter Box", "The Ghost of Muzzle Hill" and finally "The Legend of Milky Myers". Who wants to know about any of those stupid tales? All it does is stir up gossip, and the only strange thing about it is that anyone can be bothered to put it in a book at all.' Hettie tossed the volume back onto Tilly's pile of library books, looking suddenly thoughtful. She filled her catnip pipe while Tilly wrestled with the video machine, which eventually sprang into life with the promise of a horror double bill: *Devil Cat Rides Out* and *Don't Look At All*, both featuring all-star casts.

'Which one would you like first?' Tilly asked as she collected the next course and the popcorn from the table.

'The one where that dwarf cat wears a red mac' said Hettie, blowing smoke rings into the air and eyeing up a warlock tart.

Tilly clapped her paws with delight and fast-forwarded the tape to the second film. She put a generous lump of coal onto the fire and settled back on her blanket to enjoy the opening titles. The film had barely established itself when Hettie – encouraged by the catnip and a second warlock tart – interrupted her concentration. 'So what *does* she say about Milky Myers? Have you read it?'

Tilly sat up, more interested in Hettie's question than in the film's gondola funeral procession. 'I've had a quick flick through but Turner Page made it much more frightening. He said it all happened longer ago than any of us could remember.'

'Well that's a good start,' muttered Hettie. 'So much for a factual account if no one can remember. That smacks to me of making it up as you go along.'

Tilly ignored the interjection and continued. 'As you said earlier, it all happened around Miss Peggledrip's house on the outskirts of the town, where the road leads out to Much-Purring-on-the-Rug. Back then, the Myers family lived in that house. There were five of them – Mr and Mrs Myers and their three kittens, two boys and a little girl. Milky was the oldest and he helped his father with the milk round, which is how he got his name.'

Hettie began to fidget. 'That's not even interesting. Get to the good bit – weren't there lots of murders?'

'Yes, I'm getting to that, but I thought you'd like some background on the case first.'

'Oh look! There's the dwarf! Nasty little creature – wait till it turns round.'

The two cats watched as the creature in the red mac ran amok, and it was some time before they returned to the Milky Myers story.

'Now where was I?' asked Tilly, opening the toffee popcorn with such force that it scattered itself across the room. Reluctant to leave the fire, she made a mental note to gather up the stray bits in the morning and pushed on with her story as the credits rolled on *Don't Look At All*. 'They say that Milky was a bit touched.'

'Who does?' chimed in Hettie, getting irritated.

'I just did,' sighed Tilly, her patience wearing a little thin. 'Anyway, that's why he worked with his father. He couldn't be trusted to behave himself.'

Wanting to comment further but realising that Tilly wouldn't appreciate it, Hettie forced a large pawful of popcorn into her mouth and chewed as quietly as she could while her friend continued. 'One cold October morning, Milky and his father set out with their milk float to Much-Purring-on-the-Rug but they never got there, even though it was only two miles down the road. The milk float was found later that day down a farm track, with milk and broken bottles everywhere. Milky's father lay dead inside with a half empty milk bottle forced into his mouth. There was no sign of Milky, and they thought he must have been kidnapped. One of the cats from Much-Purring went to the Myers house to deliver the bad news and found the kitchen door wide open. He went in and discovered Mrs Myers and two of her kittens sitting round their breakfast table, all dead with milk bottles forced into their mouths, then he ran from the house shouting "Murder!" all the way back to Much-Purring-on-the-Rug.'

Hettie really couldn't hold herself back any longer. 'Well, that's just ridiculous! Why didn't he get help from the town? You mean to tell me that he left a dead cat in a milk float and a kitchen full of similar dead cats and ran two miles back to his village shouting "murder"? Who was this helpful bystander, or was it longer ago than anyone can remember?'

Tilly agreed that the story had wandered a little in the telling over the years, but the facts of the case were no less interesting and she pressed on. 'Later that day, Milky's aunt and uncle were discovered in the Myers dairy at the back of the house, where they worked, drowned in a large milk churn with bottles shoved in their mouths. There was still no sign of Milky. The town buried its dead and searched for months and months to find Milky, who was never seen again – well, not until years later, when a couple of kittens were playing in the garden of the empty Myers house. One of them saw a face at the window and went in to investigate. The kitten was later found dead in the back garden with a scotch egg jammed in her little mouth. To this day, no one has ever found out what happened to Milky Myers, but on Halloween his ghost returns to haunt his old house, the dairy and the farm track where the milk float was discovered, and he's also been seen in the graveyard where the Myers family were laid to rest.'

Hettie refilled her pipe and Tilly – sensing that a good conversation was about to be had – added more coal to the fire and put a pan of milk on. She noticed that a considerable amount of gravy had attached itself to the front of her cardigan; it would have to be sponged down in the morning, so while the milk came to the boil she struggled out of her day clothes into her pyjamas, returning to the fire with two steaming mugs of cocoa and Hettie's dressing gown, which she draped across the arm of her chair. Hettie kicked off her at-home slacks and jumper, and – wrapped warmly in her dressing gown – returned to her catnip.

Tilly had never been able to get on with catnip, which was a shame because the numbing properties would have helped her arthritic paws; on the rare occasions when she had taken a puff from Hettie's pipe, it just made her cough or feel sick. Hettie, on the other hand, thrived on the possibilities brought about by the mind-expanding qualities of her evening pipe, a habit gained from time on the road with her band in that almost-famous life. Her folk country-rock treatment of traditional music had left her fans spellbound, although it had to be said that most of them indulged in an evening pipe – or in some cases an all-day one – and none of her keenest followers would have considered listening to Hettie's music without the added bonus of blowing some smoke first.

The cats sipped their cocoa thoughtfully and it was Hettie who broke the silence. 'What I find odd is that everyone assumes Milky Myers murdered his own family and just disappeared, never to be seen again except as a ghost on Halloween or by a stray kitten who happened to glance up at the window of an empty house. And Irene Peggledrip has lived in that old house for as long as I can remember – she doesn't seem too worried about its history, in spite of her weird parties. And what about this cat from Much-Purring? That's a strange village at the best of times, full of halfwits with their trousers tied up with string. He had the opportunity to kill the whole of the Myers family and still be home in time for a big lunch. Maybe he killed Milky as well and no one has found the body, or even bothered to look for it.'

'Do you think he ate a scotch egg for lunch?' asked Tilly, trying to keep pace. 'That would liven the evidence up a bit.' They laughed at the ridiculous turn the story was taking, and the clock on the staff sideboard ticked towards midnight, the magical hour on Halloween when the dead rose from their graves and purveyors of dark arts stepped into the light. If there was any truth in the legend, Milky Myers would be having a very busy night.

Tilly banked up the fire, ate the last warlock tart and settled down on the fireside rug, pulling her blanket over her to keep the draught out. Hettie knocked her pipe out on the hearth, then settled back in her arm chair to watch the flames dance in the grate and cast their shadows round the room. All was well in the confines of their cosy world, and within minutes the only sound to break the silence was the contented snoring of two warm and well-fed tabby cats.

CHAPTER TWO

Tilly always awoke to the roar of the Butters' bread ovens, grateful for the warmth which they brought to the small back room. The baking day began at four in the morning, and the twin ovens worked hard to produce Betty and Beryl's famous breads, pies and pastries. The sisters had learnt their craft at their mother's kitchen table in Lancashire and had headed south with the small legacy she left them, investing in a run-down shop which was now the jewel in the crown of the town's high street. Being from the north, they had a keen work ethic, a no-nonsense approach to business, and an unpatronising kindness to those less fortunate than themselves. For obvious reasons, Hettie had been a long-standing customer of theirs, and when money was short they had always 'seen her right' with an extra pie here and there. When the great storm took her shed, the Butter sisters cleaned their back store room out and offered it to her as a bolthole; later, when fate brought Tilly to Hettie's door, the bolthole was miraculously transformed into a comfortable home, a safe haven in which to weather the storms that life chucked at them.

Tilly loved those first waking moments of each day and the security that her new life had brought her. The past had dealt some bitter blows: cruel, friendless winters; extreme hunger; and, at times, a worthless existence which could have made it so easy to give up altogether. A few kind cats had taken her in for a couple of nights or left food on their doorsteps, but until now there had been no reason to welcome a new day and what it may bring. Living with Hettie, every day was different, and they faced whatever came their way together.

It should be said, though, that no day started with both cats pulling in the same direction. Tilly knew that Hettie would never consider opening one eye, let alone two, until a cup of milky tea had been placed on the arm of her chair, and even then there was no guarantee that full consciousness could be achieved until a round of toast with a cheese triangle spread generously across it was proffered. But this morning was different: the familiar noise of the bread ovens had been replaced by an odd sort of tapping noise, and it was quite some time before Tilly realised that it was coming from the window which looked out onto the backyard. It was still very early, and as the tapping became more persistent, Tilly crept from her blanket and tugged at Hettie's right ear, the only part of her that was visible amid swathes of dressing gown and blanket.

'Wake up!' she whispered without any success. Thinking fast she tried again, this time more urgently. 'Wake up! There's a sausage and bacon roll for breakfast.' As if by magic, Hettie sat bolt upright, making a circuit of the room with her eyes and sniffing the air as if she had been snapped out of a trance by a hypnotist.

Satisfied that she had her full attention, Tilly continued. 'There's something tapping at our window – listen.'

Cross and disappointed at a no-show breakfast, Hettie grudgingly pricked up her ears, but the only obvious sound was the rumbling of her stomach. 'I can't hear anything. What are you doing up at this time anyway? If you can't sleep, read one of your library books. You early risers are a menace to society.' She continued to grumble as she pulled the blanket back over her head, and her words were lost in a tangle of bed clothes. Tilly looked at the belligerent heap of bad tempered cat, satisfied herself that the window had ceased to tap and returned to the comfort of her own blanket just as the first of the bread ovens sprang into life. Awake and alert, she reached for Marmite Sprat's interpretation of the Milky Myers case, eventually drifting back to sleep to circle the Peggledrip house in a dream. A few minutes later, she was rudely awoken again, this time by a knock at the door and the unmistakeable sound of Beryl Butter's voice.

'Wakey, wakey you two! You've got a gentleman caller. Poor lad looks a bit rough, but he's askin' for Hettie and finishin' a pie off in the yard.'

Tilly sprang from her blanket and pulled Hettie's off her chair, hoping that the shock of cold air would do the trick. This time, Hettie yawned and stretched, promising a more positive approach to the day.

'Come on! We've got to get dressed and tidy up. We've got a visitor,' Tilly explained as she folded blankets and shoved them into the staff sideboard. 'It might be a new case to work on. There's a cat in the yard asking for you. Oh, do hurry up! I'm dying to see who he is, and that explains the tapping in the night – it must be urgent if he came that early.' Tilly threw Hettie's clothes at her, crunched her way across to the table through last night's popcorn and proceeded to bring some sort of normality to the aftermath of their scary night in.

Hettie was less enthusiastic at the prospect of an unseen client in the backyard. Deep down, she hated meeting people and would have lived in a very small bubble if she'd had any choice, but good cases that paid well were hard to come by and their coffers were running low; a boost from the backyard was just what they needed. She pulled on her clothes, pushed her armchair back from the fire and riddled the coals into life, adding some kindling to cheer things up. Then, in a rare moment of domesticity, she filled the kettle at the sink, switched it on and rinsed their cocoa mugs, adding what they called their clients' cup to the tea tray. By this time, Tilly had completed the transformation from bedsit to office and had climbed into a business cardigan and some understated woolly socks, ready to receive their caller. She lifted the blind cautiously on a bright, frosty morning, shivering at the memory of all those winters out in the cold, waiting for the library to open so that she could thaw out on one of the radiators. It was there that she had discovered her love of books and her appetite for detective fiction, always knowing that at the end of each working day she would be turned out to search for a safe place to sleep.

A movement in the corner of the Butters' yard brought Tilly back from a place she rarely allowed herself to go. 'I don't think he's going to make our fortune,' she said, a little deflated. 'Just look at him! Rough isn't the word for it, and a fighter, too, I'd say.'

The battered old cat had found the only shaft of sunlight to be had in the yard and was making some attempt to clean himself after devouring a Butters' pie.

Hettie looked closer, then suddenly ran from the room with Tilly in hot pursuit.

'I don't believe it!' Hettie cried in the direction of this skinny bag of bones. 'I thought you were dead! They told me the storm had done for you.' She threw her arms round her unexpected visitor, doing a good job of crushing him to death.

'Hey, leave off! No need fer all that,' said the old cat, struggling to free himself from Hettie's welcome. 'I was in the area and I thought I'd look yer up for old time's sake. And who's this pretty ball of fluff?' The cat turned his attention to Tilly, who was hiding behind Hettie, too shy to take part in the grand reunion.

Hettie responded with full introductions, pulling Tilly out by her cardigan. 'This is my very best friend, Tilly Jenkins. Tilly, this is an old friend from my shed days, Mr Bruiser Venutius.'

Bruiser took Tilly's paw and bowed low enough for his substantial whiskers to touch the ground. 'I'm very pleased to meet yer,' he said with a wink. 'Any friend of Hettie's is a true friend o' mine.'

Tilly chuckled shyly, delighted with the gentlemanly attentions which contrasted so sharply with the cat's appearance. Beneath the dirt he was a mostly white cat, his dense short fur distinguished by stripes of black and grey, but it was the battle scars that gave him away: the one and a half ears, the smile that lacked some teeth, the eye swollen and half-closed – all bore testimony to the fact that he was indeed a fighter and, as his warrior surname implied, a winner too. His skin sagged across his bones, suggesting that a much bigger cat would emerge if he had access to regular meals, and Tilly's first instinct was to rush back inside and put the toast on whilst trying to remember how many cheese triangles they had left.

With a strange reluctance, Bruiser followed the two cats into the hallway. Once inside, he kept close to the walls, eyeing up the bread ovens with great suspicion as he trailed Hettie and Tilly to their room. The fire won him over instantly: in one agile leap, he positioned himself in front of it with his back to the heat, allowing his old bones a much-needed thaw from the night's frost.

Hettie moved over to close the door, wanting to block out the noise of the bread ovens; seeing Bruiser become suddenly agitated, she changed her mind. 'Still can't stand being shut in then?' she said as Tilly launched the bread knife into one of Betty's finest bloomers.

Bruiser nodded in an embarrassed sort of way. 'Not too keen on four walls and a closed door,' he admitted. 'I still needs me freedom – only thing I got that's mine. But a proper fire, now that's a reason to come in now and again, specially when the wood's too wet to build me a fire out under the stars.'

There was now a hive of activity around the toaster,

which in many ways was as independent as Bruiser: it was good at burnt or not cooked at all, but golden brown was a big ask and could only be achieved by constant supervision. Tilly was the self-elected cat for the job and Hettie stood by, pulling the foil off the cheese triangles ready to spread across the toast. To her dismay, the first batch was passed straight to their visitor; to add insult to injury, the second went the same way and the residue from a cheese triangle dribbled tantalisingly from Bruiser's chin onto the fireside rug. Finally, Hettie managed to elbow her way into the breakfast run, only to discover that the cheese triangles had run out and had been replaced by a very thin scraping of butter.

Tilly looked apologetic as she chewed on an all but dry bit of toast. 'I'll have to go to Malkin and Sprinkle later to stock us up, especially as we have a guest to feed.' She beamed at Bruiser, who settled himself comfortably in Hettie's armchair.

Hettie could not help the uncharitable thoughts that were running through her head. She'd quite forgotten how Bruiser's independent lifestyle revolved around the benevolence of others, and how easily he charmed his way from one sympathetic donor to another. But she also knew that he would disappear as quickly as he had arrived, and his company was to be enjoyed while they had it.

'How about a cup of tea?' she suggested brightly,

nodding to Tilly to do the honours. 'That's if we have any tea bags or milk left.'

Tilly prepared the mugs and jotted down a short grocery list while the kettle boiled. Tuesday was her day for shopping and she combined her trip to Malkin and Sprinkle's food hall with a call on her friend, Jessie, who ran a charity shop in Cheapcuts Lane. Most of Tilly's wardrobe came from there, as well as any tasty bits of town gossip that Jessie had collected since her last visit.

Within minutes of finishing his tea, Bruiser fell into a deep sleep. Hettie knew that if he intended to stay around for a few days she would have to find him an alternative to her armchair; in any case, they couldn't keep the door open all night to pander to his claustrophobic tendencies.

'I think he'd be happier in my shed tonight. I'll go and clear a space.'

Tilly dived into the staff sideboard and, after much scrabbling and muttering, emerged with a half-finished patchwork quilt that she'd given up on the previous winter when her arthritic paws became too sore to stitch; she had intended it as a Christmas present for Hettie but settled eventually on a new catnip pipe instead.

'Look, this will keep him warm. He can have my old cushion as well – you know, the one I was sick on after my birthday tea. I sponged it down and put it in the shed for emergencies.'

The two cats left their snoring visitor and made their way down the path to the bottom of the Butters' garden, past the neatly kept flower and vegetable plots, whose occupants were now suspended in the November frost like icy elves and fairies playing at statues. Preparations for the Butters' annual bonfire party were underway in the garden, and a giant stack of old boxes and bits of wood stood tall by the compost heap, promising a good time for all. The firework display was one of the biggest in the town and a highlight of the cold autumn days; it was an event marked excitedly on the calendar by those lucky enough to receive an invitation.

Tilly pulled her cardigan closer to her as the cold began to bite, and Hettie fumbled with the shed lock that was unhelpfully frozen; it gave way at last and the friends bustled into the gloom and chaos that housed a lifetime of discarded things which they could never bear to throw away. Tilly located the cushion straight away and – with a cursory sniff – deemed it suitable for further use; after much pulling and tugging, Hettie emerged from a mountain of boxes with a small paraffin stove.

'This will do for now. I'll have to get some paraffin from Hambone's when I go for my lesson with Lazarus, but Bruiser will be fine down here with your cushion and that quilt thing. It's much better than he's been used to, by the look of him.'

Tilly's heart leapt at the mention of Lazarus

Hambone and the realisation that Tuesday was also the day that Hettie had her motorbike and sidecar lesson. They had purchased the bright red machine several weeks ago from Hambone's, the town's hardware shop and reclamation yard, where motorbikes went to die or to be reborn at the hands of Meridian Hambone's gentle giant son, Lazarus. Needing to be mobile as their detective agency took off, Hettie and Tilly had fallen head over heels for Lazarus's star buy of the week, showing little regard for the fact that neither of them had ever ridden a motorbike. Having achieved a good price and thrown in weekly lessons, Lazarus agreed to store the bike in his yard until Hettie felt confident enough to drive it away; judging by her slow progress, the machine would remain at Hambone's for some time, but Tilly turned up to as many lessons as possible so that she could ride in the sidecar. It was the most exciting treat of her week, and she'd even gone as far as naming their new set of wheels 'Miss Scarlet' after a character in her favourite board game.

'How old is Bruiser?' asked Tilly, as Hettie searched for the paraffin can.

'I don't think anyone could answer that, not even Bruiser himself – he's been around for as long as I can remember. I really thought the great storm had taken him. A lot of cats died that night, too many to count. You were so lucky to be staying with Jessie and Miss Lambert.'

Tilly nodded in agreement. Miss Lambert had befriended many a cat in need, and having adopted Jessie as a tiny kitten, she continued to offer shelter where and when it was needed to those less fortunate. Tilly had never forgotten that kindness, and although Miss Lambert now resided in an ornate Chinese urn on Jessie's mantelpiece, her guiding light was brighter than ever.

'Speaking of Miss Lambert, I must get to the shops before your lesson. I promised Jessie I'd look in on her so that we could go across to the Methodist Hall together to hear your talk.'

A number of muffled expletives filled the air in the small shed as Hettie, paraffin can in paw, tumbled out from behind an assortment of old microphone stands. Wearing the latest in cobweb headgear, she let it be known as only she could that she had quite forgotten the blot on Tuesday's landscape.

'Why the hell did I agree to it? A bunch of bored busybodies with nothing better to do, sitting round in a draughty old hall expecting to be entertained by the great and the good of the town, with nothing to offer at the end of it except an over-baked slice of Victoria sponge and a cup of over-brewed tea that's strong enough to clean the drains.'

As Hettie got into her stride, Tilly knew that if she didn't interrupt her flow they would waste the best part of the day, and she waded quickly into the new war zone.

'It's what they call a friendship club and they meet because they're lonely. They've been looking forward to your talk for weeks – you're the biggest name they've had for some time, and Jessie says there's talk of nothing else when they come into the shop. They've put posters up all over the town with your picture on, so you'll have to see it through. I'm looking forward to it and it's only a couple of hours, after all.'

Hettie, now a little calmer and fresh from Tilly's diplomatic ego massage, locked the shed with a measured amount of bad grace and strode in a resigned sort of way back up the garden path to her fate at the Methodist Hall. Bruiser was still fast asleep, so she banked up the fire and grabbed her notes for the friendship group while Tilly raided the housekeeping tin and fetched the tartan shopper on wheels which she kept by one of the bread ovens in the outer hall. Swathing themselves in scarves and woolly hats, they strode off down the High Street together, stopping off briefly to order pies for supper from the Butters' shop.

The day was bright and the winter sunshine had done its best to burn off the night's frost. The High Street was bustling with shoppers and delivery vans, and there was the usual queue spilling out onto the pavement from Lavender Stamp's post office. Lavender – subscribing to the old adage that patience was a virtue and that anything from her post office counter was worth waiting for – dealt with her clients on an individual basis, dispensing Her Majesty's stamps, postal orders and deepest sympathy cards to the townsfolk with a slow and deadly accuracy.

Hettie and Tilly made good progress but slowed their pace a little as they passed Oralia Claw's Nail Bar, a business that had become famous in the town for all the wrong reasons. Oralia's spectacular death had transformed the No. 2 Feline Detective Agency into one of the most sought-after businesses of its kind, although Hettie and Tilly turned down most of the cases offered, preferring to take on assignments that required a minimum amount of effort for a maximum amount of pay.

'Still to let, then,' noted Hettie, as the empty paraffin can she'd been swinging clanked against the peeling paintwork of the late Oralia's display window. 'You'd think some enterprising cat would have snapped it up by now.'

Tilly, disentangling one of her shopper's wheels from a stray Halloween streamer that had joined them outside Hilda Dabit's Dry Cleaners, looked up at the Nail Bar and shook her head. 'Ah well, it's just like the old Myers house – no one wanted to take that on after the murders, not until Irene Peggledrip came along. Too many ghosts, that's the trouble.'

'Oh, not that again!' said Hettie. 'Halloween is over for another year, thank goodness. Milky Myers and his ridiculous story can be laid to rest, and Irene

Peggledrip is barking mad – she probably made the story up in the first place to encourage folk to go to her strange parties.'

'She calls them séances.' Tilly's words were lost in a sudden gust of wind as Hettie strode out ahead of her towards Hambone's, not wishing to engage in any further talk of ghosts, murderers or batty old cats who talked to the dead.

Tilly had caught up by the time Hettie reached the hardware shop and they went in together to be greeted by Meridian Hambone, who sat on her high stool by the counter.

'Gawd love us if it ain't Sherlock and Whatsit! What can I sell yer today?' Meridian presided over the town's Aladdin's cave. Her shop was stocked to bursting with anything and everything that a homely cat could desire, from mops and buckets to a very upmarket line in ''lectrics', all slightly soiled and of dubious provenance – a fact which was reflected in their price and in the speed with which they were pounced upon by Meridian's regulars, who asked no questions and paid in cash.

Hettie banged her empty can down on the counter with such force that Meridian threatened to topple clean off her perch.

'If it's the paraffin yer wants, you'll 'ave to get it yerself. Lazarus has gone an' broken 'is leg. One of them big old fridges fell on 'im when he was takin' – er,

I means unloadin' – it from a lorry. Stupid great lump. Now 'e's stuck down the yard up to 'ere in plaster and no 'elp to 'is poor old Ma.' Meridian paused long enough to spit an unwanted wine gum into a strategically placed bucket and continued. ''E can't do yer lesson, if that's what yer 'ere for, although I could take yer out if yer liked.' Meridian cackled in delight at Hettie's fearful expression. 'I was sitting astride bikes afore yer granny was born! I taught Lazarus all 'e knows, and I've never been one to avoid oil and grease under me claws.'

Hettie knew that she would have to respond quickly before Meridian settled into the highs and lows of her biker history. Spurred on by Tilly, who was keen to reach the food hall of Malkin and Sprinkle, she waded in. 'That's so kind of you, Meridian, and I hope Lazarus feels better soon, but I think we'll just take the paraffin today and decide what to do about the lessons later.' Hettie scrambled a collection of loose coins from her pocket and Meridian pounced on them. She retrieved the can from the counter and headed for the paraffin and oil section of the shop, noting that a bright and enticing display of fireworks was a little too close to the inflammables for comfort. Tilly, oblivious to the danger, lingered by the display, marvelling at the rockets and giant roman candles and sniffing the pungent smell of gunpowder with satisfaction.

Eyeing up the large barrel marked 'Paryfin', Hettie

began to unscrew the cap from her can while Tilly, reluctantly tearing herself away from the fireworks, seized a nearby stool and climbed onto it to reach the tap on the barrel which had a long pipe attached.

'You'll 'ave to use the funnel or it goes everywhere,' croaked Meridian from the counter, sadly too late to prevent the first half pint from tipping itself over the floor. Tilly responded fast and switched the tap to the off position, while Hettie grabbed the funnel which lay redundant on the floor and jammed it into the can. She gave Tilly the nod to open the tap again, and the cats left the successfully filled can by the counter, ready to collect on their way back from the Methodist Hall.

The shopping had to be done at speed now that it was getting late. Reluctantly, Hettie took charge of the tartan shopper and saved a place in the checkout queue, while Tilly scooted round with a trolley that had a mind of its own and rolled towards the pre-packed meat counter every time she let go of it. Eventually she re-joined Hettie, much to the disgust of those behind her in the queue – not because she had pushed in, but because the strong smell of paraffin did not mix well with other purchases.

Doris Lean was on the till and gave them both short shrift as she slammed their shopping through her newly installed bleeper. She cranked up the conveyer belt to hasten their departure, only to be foiled by Mr Sprinkle, who appeared from nowhere and spent some time passing a jovial time of day with Hettie whilst giving Doris Lean a very black look. Both Mr Malkin and Mr Sprinkle owed a great debt of gratitude to the No. 2 Feline Detective Agency and Hettie and Tilly were always assured of a warm welcome in the store, whether they reeked of paraffin or not.

With the tartan shopper fully loaded and Doris Lean put firmly in her place, Hettie and Tilly headed for Cheapcuts Lane, sharing a large packet of crisps as they went. Jessie's charity shop was opposite the Methodist Hall and Hettie could see that the keener Friendship Club members were already beginning to arrive.

'For goodness' sake, just look at them! Talk about God's waiting room. Why did I ever agree to this?'

Tilly giggled. 'Well, you're here now so you'll have to go through with it. I'll see you in there when I've picked Jessie up.' Tilly gave Hettie a gentle shove in the direction of her audience and made her way to Jessie's shop, where her friend was busy changing the window display from Halloween to bonfire night.

'Oh good, you're here. That means I can put the kettle on,' Jessie said, as she clambered out of her window display brandishing a giant knitted pumpkin. 'This'll have to go away for another year. One more week and I'll be getting the Christmas stuff out.'

Tilly loved her friend's enthusiasm for making her charity shop a magical world of colour, with themed window displays, co-ordinated clothes rails – mostly in reds, as this was Jessie's favourite colour – and a fine collection of bric-a-brac for which any department store would have killed. Tilly occasionally looked after the shop when Jessie had other business to attend to, and was paid handsomely in cardigans and other fashion knits for her trouble – which to Tilly was no trouble at all.

'Isn't Hettie coming in?' asked Jessie, giving Tilly a hug. 'I thought her talk was at two.'

'It is, but she likes to make sure the microphone's working and the treasurer has made the cheque out properly. I think it goes back to her days in music – there was a lot of trouble getting paid in those days. She often talks about being ripped off.'

Jessie laughed. 'I don't think there's any chance of that with the Methodists, but they are an odd lot. I'll have a stampede in here when their meeting breaks up later – they're very good for business. Let's have a cup of tea, then I'll shut up shop for a bit so we can go across and give Hettie some moral support.'

CHAPTER THREE

The Methodist Hall had seen much better days. On the few occasions that Hettie had had cause to visit, she had marvelled at how it always smelt of over-boiled cabbage, even though the small kitchen at the back had never served anything more adventurous than tea or coffee. All the foods that could be described as edible were brought in by the faithful on trays under tea towels or in plastic sealed boxes.

Today was no different. As Hettie made her way through the main door, she was virtually ignored by a bevy of cats clustered round a trestle table at the back of the hall next to the kitchen hatch. They were busy laying out their baking in a competitive spirit that would have won wars: the obligatory Victoria sponge was jostling for position with a fussy mound of chocolate icing that had once been a Swiss roll; the scones looked quite nice, but the currants were burnt; and the porridge oat flapjacks were forced to remain in their plastic container, as no amount of coaxing could free them from the sticky mess of surplus syrup that had oozed out in transit.

'Ah, Miss Bagshot! Welcome, welcome, welcome to our little Friendship Club! I'm so pleased you have found time to be with us for our Tuesday gathering. We are honoured to have such an important visitor in our midst. I spoke with you on the phone. I am Miss Anderton – that's Bugs Anderton to my close friends.'

Hettie stood rooted to the spot as the Scottish ginger cat sailed across the hall towards her, only faltering when the paraffin smell filled her meeter-and-greeter's nostrils. Seeing that the spillage was still causing a problem, and worried that her personal hygiene would be under discussion at the next meeting, Hettie responded to her welcome. 'I must apologise for the smell on my clothes,' she said. 'My colleague and I have just returned from an undercover surveillance job where paraffin was stored, and I didn't want to be late for the talk so there was no time to go home and change.'

'My dear Miss Bagshot! How terribly exciting!

Fancy, you've come to us fresh – er, straight – from a real case! This can only add to the success of the afternoon. If you would care to freshen up in the members' cloakroom, I'll get Miss Treemints – our head of beverages – to make you a nice cup of tea. There's no rush, as we have one or two matters of club business to get through before you're called upon, and we're waiting for stragglers to arrive before we can begin.'

Hettie followed directions to the cloakroom and took some time to wash her paws with a large bar of carbolic soap that had probably been in the building since it was built. The roller towel had been round the block a few times, too, and she decided to wipe her paws on her slacks instead. The paraffin smell was still there, but the carbolic soap had done its best to overpower it. Confident that she was now ready to meet her public, she gave herself a sideways glance in the cracked mirror and ventured back out into the hall to be met by a nervous looking cat proffering a cup of very strong tea which rattled on its saucer.

'Miss Anderton asked me to make this for you. I hope there's enough milk in it. I wasn't sure how you liked it.'

Hettie offered a full smile as she took control of the tea. 'That's lovely,' she lied. 'Just the way I like it, Miss . . . er?'

'Treemints. Delirium Treemints, head of beverages

and embroidered kneelers, although we don't make those any more. Miss Anderton thinks they have gone out of fashion.'

Hettie was cautious in her response, mainly because she had no conversation regarding kneelers of any sort and she had noticed that Delirium's paw was still shaking even though she was relieved of the tea. Bugs Anderton came to the rescue, clapping her paws together and calling the Friendship Club to order. Delirium scuttled away to take up her chair by the refreshments hatch, leaving Hettie to make her way forward to where Bugs Anderton was patting a chair on the small stage.

Hettie took her place next to the club's president as Tilly and Jessie crept in at the back, giving her the paws-up sign as they settled into their seats. It was, however, some time before Hettie took centre stage. Bugs Anderton rose to her full height, stretching her long ginger neck to reveal elegant darker stripes, a signal to the faithful that she was about to speak. She tapped the microphone, satisfying herself that none of her words would be lost, and the Methodist Hall fell silent as all eyes turned to the stage. Bugs paused for dramatic effect, enjoying the power of expectation, and then began. 'Members and friends, I am delighted to . . .'

A crash came from the back of the hall and a large cardboard box burst through the door as if on a gust of wind. It was propelled by a thin, bespectacled dark brown cat, and seventeen pairs of eyes turned to watch Marmite Sprat make her late and very ill-timed entrance, more public than she had hoped.

Bugs Anderton was not amused. In fact, the hackles on her elegant neck were there for all to see as the seventeen pairs of eyes returned their gaze to the stage, which Hettie hoped in vain might open up and swallow them all.

'Miss Sprat,' Bugs boomed, trying to regain control of the situation, 'I'm sure we're all very pleased that you are able to honour us with your presence today, but you are well aware of our commencement time and according to my watch it is three minutes past two. I suggest you put your box down and quickly occupy a vacant chair at the back of the hall so that we may continue without further ado.'

Marmite faltered, then opened her mouth to speak, but Bugs was ahead of her and raised her paw as a barrier to any further interruption. Marmite allowed the box to slide to the floor and slunk into the first vacant chair she could find.

With the seat of power re-established, Bugs began again. 'Members and friends, I am delighted to welcome Miss Bagshot into our midst today as our speaker. Miss Bagshot, as you may know, is the proprietor of the No. 2 Feline Detective Agency and has come to indulge us on how we may keep our valuables safe. There will, of course, be an opportunity for members to ask questions from the floor. I'm sure we would all like to know a little more about some of the more . . . shall we say colourful cases she has been professionally involved in, wouldn't we?'

The Friendship Club responded as one with a polite audible 'Yes.' Hettie fidgeted, eyeing up the crowd and taking in for the first time how diverse the gathering was. There were a few familiar faces – stalwarts of the town with claws in many pies, the flag sellers and bucket collectors who peppered the High Street on charity days, one or two members of the Pawlights local drama group and a few elderly cats who looked like they'd just come out for the afternoon to feel the warmth of the old cast iron radiators dotted around the hall. Hettie's eyes eventually rested on Marmite Sprat – thin, pinched, and as far as Hettie could see, with no endearing physical qualities at all. Everything about Marmite was sharp and pointed; even her glasses had wings that stuck out from her face, reminding Hettie of the knives on Ben-Hur's chariot, a film she often had to watch as it was one of Tilly's favourites.

Bugs had been speaking for some time, and Hettie pulled herself back to the present just in time to realise that there was another hitch in the afternoon meeting of the Friendship Club.

'And now I call on Mavis Spitforce for the minutes of our last meeting,' the president continued. 'Come on Mavis, we haven't got all day.' Heads swivelled. Hettie scanned the audience and saw straight away that Miss Spitforce wasn't there; she had taken on a small case for her several weeks ago and they had enjoyed a number of afternoon teas together in the course of her investigations.

'Does anyone know why Mavis isn't here?' demanded Bugs, whose patience was looking increasingly frayed at the edges. The sea of faces shook their heads as one. 'Very well. This is highly irregular, but it seems that I must read the minutes myself.'

Hettie glanced at the sheets of paper that Bugs Anderton was shuffling into some kind of order, wondering why she'd had to call on someone else to read them in the first place. She also noticed that the 'minutes' ran into several pages and cheered up at the prospect of giving a shorter talk herself. Bugs cleared her throat, indicating that she was about to begin.

'The meeting of the last Methodist Hall Friendship Club was held on Tuesday 25th October. The meeting was opened by the club president, Miss Bugs Anderton, who informed us that the membership fees would be increased as and with effect from 1st November, due to the annual increase in the hire of the Methodist Hall. It was decided to look for cheaper premises for the New Year, when the membership list would also be reviewed. Miss Anderton announced that the Christmas lunch would be held in the restaurant of Malkin and Sprinkle on 12th December and that all members should pay for their places at the next meeting, when a menu would be made available with a choice of main course. All money to be paid to our treasurer, Miss Balti Dosh. Miss Anderton also informed us that the after-lunch entertainment would, this year, be a performance of best loved Christmas carols and other seasonal novelties, presented by the combined spoon players and bell ringing club from Much-Purring-on-the-Rug.'

Hettie took another look at the crowd, keen to locate the treasurer, and settled on a very pretty Asian cat wearing a bright pink sari who smiled at the mention of her name.

'Miss Anderton then informed us that the guest speaker for the next meeting would be Miss Hettie Bagshot of the No. 2 Feline Detective Agency. Captain Lionel Standback then took the stage and gave us an enlightening talk on bomb disposal, after which members were invited to vote on the best crocheted bookmark. The winner for the third year in succession – by a unanimous vote – was Miss Bugs Anderton, who received a standing ovation before tea was served by Delirium Treemints, assisted by Hilary Fudge and her daughter Cherry. The chairs were then neatly stacked by . . .'

Hettie began to feel that the Friendship Club had turned into some sort of purgatory from which she would never be allowed to escape. The 'minutes' seemed to grow into days, weeks and then years, and it was a bit of a shock when Bugs Anderton finally announced her name to a round of relieved and eager applause. Knowing now that there was a real glimmer of hope at the end of the tunnel, Hettie rose from her chair, adjusted the microphone to suit her height, and began.

'Paws up anyone here who has been burgled or had their pocket picked,' she said. The response was slow, but eventually Delirium, Balti and the Fudges raised their paws. 'Well, as you can see, it's not uncommon and these days it happens more and more.' In truth, Hettie had absolutely no idea where she was going with this but she ploughed on, waiting for Bugs Anderton to signal the end of the talk and the beginning of the question and answer session. 'The best thing to do with your valuables is to keep them safe and not let anybody know you've got them in the first place – that way, no one will want to steal them. If you have expensive jewellery, try not to wear it when you go out and never hide it in the same place twice as someone might be watching. A strong padlock is a very good idea if you have a shed or garage full of treasures, but you must remember where you've put the key or you might not be able to get in yourself.' Hettie paused as Balti Dosh let out a loud chuckle, inspiring some nervous tittering which gave her vital seconds to beef up her presentation. 'Assume that every stranger you meet is a thief. Never reveal how much money you have in your purse at a shop counter, and always look behind you on a dark night to make sure no one is following you – they may attack you and leave you for dead in an alleyway. If you hear a noise in the night, stay quiet or hide under the bed until the intruder has gone – make a sound, and he may hear you and silence you for good.'

Hettie's talk was becoming a little too dark for some of the older members, and Bugs came to everyone's rescue – including Hettie's – by offering a vote of thanks before signalling to Delirium Treemints to fire up the tea urn.

'I'm sure Miss Bagshot would be happy to answer one or two questions before tea. Who would like to go first?'

Balti Dosh shot an eager paw into the air, warming to the darker subject matter. 'Please, Miss Bagshot – is it true that you ran someone through with a kebab skewer at Malkin and Sprinkle?'

Bugs Anderton rose from her chair, unplugging the microphone with one swift movement before Hettie had a chance to respond. 'Sadly we are out of time,' she shouted, completely wrong-footed by her treasurer. 'May I remind members that Miss Balti Dosh is collecting your money for the Christmas lunch? Menus have been pinned up at the back of the hall and Marmite Sprat will be selling copies of her latest collection of *Strange But Trues* during the tea interval.' Bugs Anderton then turned to Hettie and spoke in a much more discreet tone. 'Miss Bagshot, please let me apologise on behalf of the Friendship Club for Miss Dosh's inappropriate question. I can see she has upset you. I'm afraid she has a rather . . . er . . . lurid view of life. In fact, I had to ask her to give up her post as entertainments officer when she organised a trip to go behind the scenes of the crematorium. Not my idea of a day out, I must say.'

With her apology made, Bugs left the stage, signalling that the show was over. There was much scraping of chairs as the Friendship Club stood up, some breaking away to ponder the menus for their Christmas treat, others manning the cake table where Delirium was pairing off the cups and saucers ready to dispense the tea. Balti Dosh stood with cash box and clipboard, poised to receive contributions from those who were signing up for the festive lunch. More than a little shell-shocked, Hettie remained in her seat as Tilly and Jessie made their way to the front.

'Blimey!' Jessie said. 'What a question to ask! Some people have no tact whatsoever.'

'In fairness, I think she was just being enthusiastic,' said Hettie. 'She wasn't to know that it was one of the worst moments of my life.'

'The kebabs tasted good though,' chimed in Tilly,

doing her best to lighten the situation. She succeeded, and the three friends burst out laughing.

While Bugs Anderton had what appeared to be a serious conversation with her treasurer, Delirium Treemints made her way to the stage with a laden tray of tea and cake for Hettie and her party. In spite of the rattling and Delirium's nerves, it might have been delivered successfully were it not for the arrival of Teezle Makepeace shouting 'MURDER!' at the top of her voice. The crockery crashed to the floor, and the Methodist Hall fell silent as all eyes turned towards the new arrival.

Teezle Makepeace had been the town's post-cat for several years, larger-than-life in all senses of the word and loved by all, not just for the fact that you could set your watch by her two deliveries a day, but also for her keen interest in the community in general.

Teezle always seemed to have time for a cup of tea and a chat with some of the more neglected cats on her rounds, and she could turn her paw to all sorts of helpful little jobs like changing light bulbs, filling coal scuttles and sweeping snow from paths. Perhaps the most remarkable thing about her, though, was that she had managed to find favour with the Post Mistress, Lavender Stamp, who – until taking her on – had managed to get through an average of two post-cats a month.

Today was clearly a day that Teezle would remember

for the rest of her life. Bugs pulled herself away from her conversation with Balti, irritated by yet another calamity poised to derail the November meeting.

'Miss Makepeace! Whatever do you mean by such a dramatic entrance? Murder is not a word to be used lightly in the Methodist Hall.'

Teezle, it seemed, had no time to stop and chat. It was Hettie she was seeking, and – having located her at the other end of the Hall – she pushed unceremoniously past Bugs.

'Hettie, thank goodness I've found you! You must come with me – the most terrible thing has happened. I went straight to your office when I found her but there was an old cat I didn't know watching your TV, so I asked one of the Butters and she pointed to a poster in their shop. I hightailed it down here hoping you hadn't left yet. I locked her door and took the key in case someone called on her. They wouldn't want to see her like that. It's awful and all done up for Halloween. I thought she'd made a Guy for bonfire night, then I realised it was her.'

Teezle gulped for air, giving Hettie the space she needed to get a word in edgeways. 'Start from the beginning. Who are you talking about?'

'It's Miss Spitforce. She's dead!'

Delirium Treemints had been collecting up the broken crockery from her abortive tea run, but on hearing the news she fainted clean away in a puddle of tea and Victoria sandwich. Tilly and Jessie dragged her to one side to allow Hettie and Teezle some space and left her in the capable paws of Hilary and Cherry Fudge, the Club's elected first-aiders. Seeing that a new incident had taken place, the Friendship Club began to converge on the stage end of the hall, leaving only Marmite Sprat with a table of unsold books, and Bugs Anderton, who for the first time was seriously considering resigning her presidency and going to live by the sea.

'We need to get out of here,' said Jessie, fighting her way through the crowd. 'Let's go across to my shop – it'll be easier to talk there.' Hettie nodded in agreement, and Jessie led them out of the scrum and into the peace and quiet of her parlour. She made a pot of hot, sweet tea and sat quietly with Tilly, while Hettie gently coaxed Teezle into sharing her account of the discovery of Mavis Spitforce's body.

'I was doing my afternoon deliveries and I'd got to Whisker Terrace. Mr Dosh came out of his shop and asked if I'd like a couple of samosas for my tea – they were a bit past their date, but he knows they're my favourite and he's nice like that. Anyway, I already had a chop in for my tea so I decided to offer a samosa to Miss Spitforce. I did a couple more deliveries and got to her house at about two o'clock, then I remembered it was her afternoon at the Friendship Club so I decided to put her samosa and a couple of letters in her back porch – she always leaves it open, you see. That's when I saw her. The porch leads into the kitchen and the door was wide open. I thought it was a dummy to start with, then I looked more closely and . . .' A giant sob swallowed the rest of the sentence.

Hettie knew they would get no further while Teezle was in such a state; the only way to piece together what had happened was to go and see for herself.

'I think we'd better pay a visit to Miss Spitforce's,' she said, nodding to Tilly to make a move.

Suddenly, their peace was shattered by a thunderous banging from Jessie's shop. 'Oh, for goodness' sake,' Jessie said, parting her beaded door curtain. 'You'd think they'd want to go straight home after such a nightmare of an afternoon. Look at them clambering to get at the bric-a-brac! I'll have to let them in or they'll batter the door down. Stay as long as you like and let yourselves out the back when you're ready. Let me know how things are later.' Jessie made her way through to the shop and shot the bolt across, opening the floodgates on the hordes of Babylon – or, more especially, on the fallout from the Methodist Hall.

CHAPTER FOUR

Whisker Terrace was in a very pleasant part of the town, far enough away from the High Street to afford its residents some peace and quiet, but close enough for shopping without the bus. The terrace also boasted its own convenience store, run by Rogan Dosh and his family and highly valued by the Whisker Terrace community, which was largely made up of reasonably well-off elderly cats. Rogan and his much younger wife, Balti, toiled day and night to provide necessities like tea, bread and milk long after the bigger stores had brought their shutters down for the day. They had also introduced a delicious array of Asian foods to the communities they served, and cats travelled significant distances for one of Balti's home-made chicken tikka masalas, cooked in huge vats and packaged in foil trays with lids for easy transportation. Balti's teenage son, Bhaji, had even followed in the family's tradition of hard work and enterprise by starting a delivery service on his bicycle.

Hettie, Tilly and Teezle rounded the corner into Whisker Terrace, nearly bumping into Balti, who had obviously decided against a raid on Jessie's bric-a-brac and was sweeping the front of her shop in a frenetic sort of way.

'Ah, Miss Bagshot, please let me say how very sorry I am to have upset you this afternoon. It's not every day that one meets a real detective and I am most interested in all aspects of true crime, but I'm afraid I get a little carried away at times. I hope you will forgive me.' Balti's gaze fell on Teezle, who had been hiding behind Hettie, hoping not to be dragged into the conversation. 'Oh my goodness! Has there been a real murder? I thought it was all a jolly joke at the club, you know – to liven things up.' Hettie decided that further discussion with Balti could in no way improve the afternoon, and was about to make a polite excuse for moving on when Bhaji appeared from nowhere and crash-landed his bicycle into a tub of flowers outside the shop. His mother paused in her apology to box his ears, enabling Hettie to lead her party onward to the grim business that awaited them next door at number 19.

Hettie had spent a number of pleasant afternoons in the company of Mavis Spitforce, having agreed to investigate a series of odd events in Mavis's garden shortly after the traumas of the now famous Furcross case. The puzzle was an ideal distraction from the horror that Balti Dosh had alluded to at the Friendship Club, and Mavis Spitforce was an interesting and wise old cat who had unwittingly helped Hettie to get the darker memories of Furcross into perspective – so it was with great trepidation and sadness that she opened the door of Miss Spitforce's porch.

'I locked the back door so no one could see her,' said Teezle, proffering a key. 'She's sitting at her kitchen table.'

Hettie put the key in the lock and looked back at her two companions. Tilly had said very little for some time, and Hettie could see that she was anxious and frightened at what they might find; Teezle, too, was shaking uncontrollably, but in her case the reaction came from knowledge rather than imagination.

'Look you two, there's no need for us all to have nightmares,' Hettie said. 'Tilly, why don't you take Teezle back to ours and make sure she's all right? I'll see what's to be done here and join you later.'

Tilly responded immediately, pleased to be given an important job and relieved not to have to come face to face with 'poor Miss Spitforce', as Mavis would forever now be known. 'We'll go by the High Street,' she said, taking Teezle's arm. 'That way we can pick up the paraffin from Hambone's. It's getting frosty already and Bruiser will be cold in that shed.'

Hettie waved them off with the tartan shopper and went back into the porch, this time turning the key in the lock. Pausing to take a deep breath, she opened the door. The scene was not immediately one of horror. In fact, the cat sitting at the kitchen table was almost comedic at first glance, appearing to have come straight from a rather good Halloween fancy dress party; on closer inspection, though, Hettie realised that whoever had done this to Mavis Spitforce had been very serious indeed.

Tearing her eyes away from the corpse for a moment, Hettie allowed herself to take in her surroundings. The bright, warm kitchen was the same as she remembered it, and nothing was out of place except the postbag which lay on the floor by the door where Teezle had abandoned it. There was no sign of a struggle, just the everyday trappings of an elderly cat's kitchen. Turning back to the body, she noticed that it was sitting forward on the chair, with the table holding it in place. Mavis's head wore a witch's hat and an eye mask which Hettie carefully removed to reveal two very dead, staring eyes. She tried to close them to give Miss Spitforce some dignity, but numerous attempts only succeeded in disturbing the body: the hat toppled to the floor and so did the corpse, dislodging itself from the table and falling flat on its face to reveal an elaborate dagger sunk squarely between Miss Spitforce's shoulder blades. Most of the blood had been soaked up by an orange silk cloak. The cloak had been thrown around the body after death, Hettie noticed: the dagger had not pierced the material as it entered the victim. She tried to control the panic that was welling up inside her. Staring down at the pathetic heap of orange silk, she saw a stain gradually spreading across it, and it was a moment or two before she realised that the mark was caused by her own tears.

She backed away, wiping her eyes and blowing her nose on a tea towel by the sink. For a long time, she stared out of the kitchen window, searching in the gathering November gloom for some strength and composure. She thought back to her tea time chats with Mavis Spitforce: hadn't she talked of a niece, of whom she was very fond? And a sister? Yes, there was definitely a sister. They would both have to be told. Mavis needed her family at this time, while Hettie got to the bottom of who was responsible and why the elderly cat had been killed in such a cruel way.

Feeling stronger, she turned back to the body and in one courageous movement retrieved the dagger from Miss Spitforce's shoulder blades and placed it on the tear-stained tea towel. Quickly, she removed all the

Halloween trappings from the body to reveal the cat she had known: trim, respectable, and – even in death – neatly turned out in a heather mixture twin set.

Hettie had never been further than the kitchen on her previous visits, but knew that she would have to find a suitable place to leave the body. There was a small parlour next door, neat and tidy and full of books, with a desk in the corner by the window, a Chinese lamp on a side table, and an ornate but well-used chaise longue in front of the fireplace. Hettie was satisfied that Miss Spitforce could reside there until arrangements were made. She returned to the kitchen with that in mind just as the hammering began on the front door. Mavis was clearly in no fit state to receive visitors and Hettie decided to ignore the intrusion and carry on with her 'tidying up' when the kitchen door burst open and a whirlwind entered in an oversized great coat, yellow wellingtons and a Cossack hat jammed firmly on her head.

'Stay where you are!' she hissed, misunderstanding the situation. 'You won't get away with this.'

Hettie froze for a second, then relaxed as she recognised the considerable form of Irene Peggledrip, who fancied herself as the town's practitioner of the darker arts.

'Miss Peggledrip,' she said, 'I am Hettie Bagshot from the No. 2 Feline Detective Agency. I was called here by Teezle Makepeace, who discovered the body of poor Miss Spitforce and asked for my help.'

'No need to call me "Peggledrip" – it's a ridiculous name. Irene will do. That's I-RE-NE – three syllables and don't forget it.'

Hettie was a little taken aback by Miss Peggledrip's response and wondered why she wasn't more shocked by the news of Mavis Spitforce's death; there was, of course, an obvious explanation, and she was about to hear it.

'I knew it! Crimola is never wrong about these things. I should have come this morning, but poor Mr Bunch wanted to speak with his wife. He's been looking for the tin opener since she passed on, poor old cat. He's lost without her, although I can tell you she's having a high old time. Crimola says she's the life and soul, if you'll pardon the expression.'

Irene Peggledrip pulled a chair out from the kitchen table, divested herself of her Cossack hat and settled in as if waiting for the kettle to boil. As she clearly had some information with a bearing on the case, Hettie felt obliged to join her.

'Miss Peggledr . . . er . . . Irene – are you telling me that someone called Crimola told you that Miss Spitforce was dead?'

'Not someone exactly, just Crimola. She lives in my head and sends me messages. I don't really think of her as a person, but she keeps me up to date with stuff going on – on the other side, if you see what I mean.' Hettie nodded, not wishing to interrupt and needing to get to the stage where she could find a small moment of sanity in which to remove Miss Spitforce from her kitchen floor. 'I was enjoying a late supper last night,' Irene Peggledrip continued. 'Sardines on toast, actually. I'd just finished reading that stupid cat's book on the goings-on in my house. Preposterous nonsense! She's got a damned cheek, if you ask me. Anyway, Crimola comes through all agitated and says Mavis has just turned up. I thought that was a bit odd as she called round yesterday afternoon. In fact, it was she who brought me Marmite Sprat's book. She was keen on the so called "Milky Myers" case and I think she was planning to write a proper account of it. She told me there were a few questions that she'd like me to put to Crimola when we had our next session.'

Hettie was hanging on but felt that she needed to clarify a few things before allowing Irene Peggledrip to continue. 'You say that Miss Spitforce was also writing a book on the Myers case? Did she say what she thought to Marmite Sprat's version of the story?'

'Rubbish! That's what she said, and after I'd read it I had to agree with her. I won't deny that I've got an interesting lot of spirits floating about my old place, but Crimola sifts the good from the bad and none of them bother me too much. It's best to leave the difficult ones alone, though. I like to think of them as being shut away in a freezer. Anyway, that's why

Mavis wanted to book a session with Crimola – to check up on some facts.'

Hettie was a little confused. 'But you said that Crimola lives in your head, so why did Miss Spitforce need to book a session with her? Why didn't she just talk to you there and then?'

'Ah, bless you! The conditions have to be right for Crimola to speak. She has to take me over for a bit, and that's a full on session. She channels herself through me and I only tend to do that sort of work on Fridays.'

'But you said you'd helped Mr Bunch find his tin opener this morning and it's Tuesday, so how does that work?' asked Hettie, her irritation made worse by the first pangs of hunger; the shared packet of crisps was just a distant memory.

'Well, I didn't find the tin opener actually. She'd thrown it away before she passed over as she didn't want him living on that nasty tinned stuff. But I went straight to her and it was a simple job – no need to involve Crimola in that one.'

Hettie was keen to move things along: it was getting late and Mavis was still taking up most of her kitchen floor.

'Would you help me to make Miss Spitforce a little more comfortable? I think she'd be better in the parlour.'

Irene Peggledrip smiled. 'Of course I will, but

she's not here any more. My guess is she left around midnight and she's being processed as we speak. I'll know more in a day or two. Why don't you come and see me on Friday? Crimola may have some answers for you.'

For some unknown reason, Hettie agreed to the somewhat bizarre assignation with Crimola and the two cats bore Mavis Spitforce's body into her parlour, leaving her in peaceful repose on the chaise longue. Having waved off her new friend, Cossack hat and all, Hettie picked up Teezle's bag of abandoned letters, took one last look at the murder scene and locked the door, knowing that she would have to return in the morning to do some real detective work.

She made her way down the passageway and back onto Whisker Terrace, and then stopped dead; there was something she needed to check and it wouldn't wait for the morning. Letting herself back in, she went straight to the parlour and to the corpse. She looked down on Miss Spitforce's face and noticed a slight bulge in her cheeks. Taking great care not to break the jaw, Hettie gently prised the mouth open wide enough to see that there was more than teeth inside. She looked round for something to help and settled on a pair of tweezers that had been left on the desk, tweezers which Miss Spitforce had used to add to her butterfly collection, a hobby she was very keen on.

Returning to her grim task, she removed several

small bits of paper from the victim's mouth; on closer inspection, it was clear that the fragments related to the Milky Myers story and – by the quality of the paper – had come from Marmite Sprat's *Strange But True* version of events. She put the fragments in a convenient jar on the mantelpiece, secured the house once again and strode off home, hoping for a good dinner, a blazing fire and a pipe or two of catnip.

Those hopes were shattered when she arrived home to a less than blissful scene. Her arrival went unnoticed, mainly due to the volume of the TV, and only after she'd banged the door shut did Tilly react, shrugging her shoulders in a desperately apologetic way as if the chaos was none of her making. She got up from her blanket and bounded over the considerable bulk of Teezle Makepeace, who was lying stretched out in front of the fire, singing along with Bruiser, who was still in Hettie's chair. They were glued to a rerun of *Top of the Cats*, and – to make things worse – a number of empty plates were dotted round as if a good time had been had by all.

'I'm so sorry,' Tilly said, seeing the look on Hettie's face. 'There was nothing I could do. Teezle said she needed to eat because her blood sugar was dropping with the shock, whatever that means, and Bruiser had already collected our dinner from the Butters when I got back and eaten most of it. I felt obliged to give the rest of it to Teezle, and now they seem to have settled in for the evening.'

'Well, that's what they think! Just follow my lead, but hang on to Teezle – I need to have a quick word with her before she goes.' Hettie acted swiftly, pulling the TV plug out of the socket to cut short Teezle and Bruiser's backing vocals to *I Will Survive* and bring the impromptu party to an end. 'Sorry about that,' she said, 'but we've a very important client calling in on us this evening and I'm afraid you'll have to make yourselves scarce.'

Tilly marvelled at Hettie's ingenuity and played her part by scurrying around collecting the empty plates, folding her blanket and fetching Teezle's coat. Bruiser stretched and yawned.

'Well, I s'pose I'd better make a move. 'Spect it's a cold old night out there, and I'd better find me a bit o' shelter afore the frost settles.'

Hettie spotted the paraffin can by the door. 'No need for that, Bruiser. You can stay in our shed for as long as you like. There are cushions and blankets and we picked up some paraffin for the old stove – you'll be snug in there.' Hettie was doing her best to sound hospitable but inside she was seething; after the day she'd had, the last thing she needed was an overweight post-cat and a stray from her past clogging up the fireside.

Bruiser sprang from Hettie's chair and followed

her out into the backyard, keen to be settled in for the night. Hettie returned minutes later as Teezle Makepeace was about to leave.

'Before you go, Teezle, I need your help. Miss Spitforce mentioned that she had a sister and a niece – we need to get in touch with them. I don't suppose they're on your post round?'

Teezle's face lit up at the thought of assisting in the investigation. 'I know where her sister lives, but they don't get on.'

Hettie sighed. 'Well, maybe when she knows Mavis is dead they'll get on better.' It seemed an odd thing to say but it had been a long day and Hettie's reasoning was more accurate than she could have hoped.

Teezle wasn't sure whether she should laugh or not, but Tilly came to the rescue. 'Shall I jot down the address?'

'We should phone her tonight,' Hettie said. 'The sooner she knows, the better.'

Teezle shook her head. 'No chance of that. She's hardly got enough to feed herself, let alone afford a telephone. She lives in one of those tiny flats at the bottom of Cheapcuts Lane – number 7.'

Hettie sighed again. 'Well, it'll have to wait for the morning. I'll call round on my way to Miss Spitforce's. There's a lot to be done there, and I don't want anyone disturbing the crime scene until I've gathered all the evidence. I think the sister should be told, though – unless of course she knows already.'

There was a silence as the three cats looked at each other. Tilly broke the spell by reaching for her notepad and jotting down the address. Keen for Teezle to be on her way, Hettie hesitated over asking any more questions – and if she was honest, the biggest question was what was for dinner now that Teezle and Bruiser had made short work of the Butters' best steak pies – but the case had to be solved, and the post-cat was perfectly placed to supply local information.

'Before you go, Teezle, tell me what you know about Miss Spitforce. Was she well-liked in the community?'

Teezle thought for a moment. 'Well, she was always nice to me. I think some cats found her a bit scary because she was clever and always reading difficult books with long words. She liked doing those family history things, and she made big charts tracing who belonged to whom. She often had one on the go when I stopped in for a chat. She did them for her friends, I think.'

'Did you notice any particular family names in her research?' asked Hettie, not sure whether this was an interesting line of questioning or not.

'She did the Treemints – I know that because Miss Treemints was with her one day when I called in and they were both very excited because Miss Spitforce had discovered a famous actor. Beer Bone Treemints or something – he was a great, great, great uncle of Delirium's. Anyway, they were very pleased about that and Delirium was so overcome that she knocked her cup and saucer onto the floor. I helped her clear it up while Miss Spitforce made another cup of tea for us.'

Hettie couldn't help but think that Delirium Treemints spent most of her time clearing up broken crockery, regardless of her ancestors, but she pushed on as Teezle seemed keen to talk.

'Did Miss Spitforce share any of her findings with you?'

'Not really. In fact, I called in last week and she had a chart laid out on her table; she folded it up like greased lightning when she saw me, and stuck it under a cushion on one of her kitchen chairs.'

Hettie had suddenly forgotten she was hungry. Even Tilly, who had continued to take notes, moved in closer as Teezle lapped up the questions, pleased with the appreciation of her responses.

'Did Miss Spitforce ever mention that she was writing a book?'

Teezle thought again and laughed. 'She always seemed to be writing or reading something. Like I said, she was clever, but I took her post in one day and she had a parcel which she opened while I was there. It was a book. She took one look at it and threw it across the kitchen. I had to duck. It was a copy of . . .'

'. . . Marmite Sprat's *Strange But Trues*,' said Hettie, finishing Teezle's sentence.

Tilly was impressed. Teezle stared in admiration, and Hettie's hunger pains returned with a vengeance.

'One more question before you go – do you deliver to Miss Peggledrip?'

'Well, not exactly *to* her,' Teezle admitted, looking quite fearful. 'It's not a place I look forward to on my round on account of the old murder. I quite like Miss Peggledrip, though. She's a bit mad, but that old place she's got is creepy and it's the last house going out of the town. I just put her letters in the mailbox at the bottom of her drive, unless I have a parcel – then I have to take it right up to the house.'

'And what do you know about the old murder?' asked Hettie, helping Teezle on with her coat.

'Just that a cat called Milky Myers killed all his family a long time ago. Since then, he's haunted the old house and he might kill again, especially on Halloween.' Suddenly realising what she had said, Teezle gasped and put her paw up to her mouth. 'Poor Miss Spitforce! Do you think Milky Myers killed her?'

'I think that's the general idea,' said Hettie, steering Teezle to the back door. 'You've been very helpful. I may need to speak with you again, and if you think of anything else we'll be at Miss Spitforce's for most of the day tomorrow.'

Teezle said her farewells, took custody of her mail

bag and disappeared into the frost, never to be seen alive again. If Hettie had been quicker putting her coat on, she might have seen the figure loom out of the darkness in pursuit of the postcat, but it was the discussion with Tilly over who should have what from Greasy Tom's mobile food van that delayed her – and it would be some time before Teezle's body was discovered.

CHAPTER FIVE

Hettie returned to a blazing fire and a table laid out for supper. While she was stamping her feet in the cold, waiting for Greasy Tom to fry a fresh batch of sausages and bacon, Tilly had flown round their room like a dervish, putting Hettie's dressing gown to warm, laying out her pipe and catnip pouch on the arm of the chair, and filling her own hot water bottle before sliding it under her fireside blanket. A pan of milk for two large mugs of cocoa came to the boil just as Hettie stepped over the threshold.

Appreciating the sudden burst of heat that wasted no time in thawing out her whiskers, Hettie put the newspaper-wrapped parcel of food down on the table. Tilly dished it up onto two plates while Hettie pulled off her day clothes and bounded into her armchair, glad for the warmth of her dressing gown.

'Thank goodness it's all over for another day! I don't think I could take much more. Bruiser turning up in the middle of the night, Bugs Anderton and her gaggle of bloody Methodists, a corpse dressed up as a pumpkin with a dagger in her back, I-RE-NE Peggledrip and her friend Crimola stamping all over the crime scene and issuing invitations to talk to dead cats – oh and last but by no means least, Teezle Makepeace who eats us out of house and home and seems convinced that a psycho cat from longer ago than any of us can remember marauds round the town on Halloween stabbing elderly cats to death in their own homes.'

Tilly waited patiently until her friend had finished chronicling the salient points of the day, then placed a full plate of sausages and bacon in front of her and took her own plate to the fireside. The cats chewed and licked their way through their supper, gathering strength from the first decent meal they'd had all day. Full, warm and content at last, they were ready to discuss the day's events in a rational and constructive way. Hettie began by bringing Tilly up to speed with her initial observations of Miss Spitforce's body and her encounter with Irene Peggledrip.

'She's invited me to go and have a session with

Crimola on Friday. She seems to think I'll get some answers that way.'

Tilly clapped her paws excitedly. 'Ooh, do you think I could come? I've always wanted to go to one of her séances. Jessie goes once a month to speak to Miss Lambert. She says Miss Peggledrip has a real talent.'

'Yes, I bet she does,' said Hettie, more sarcastically than she intended. 'But I can't help feeling that allowing Crimola to solve all our cases might just put us out of a job. I definitely think you should tag along, though – I'll need you to take notes and keep your eyes peeled. If Miss Peggledrip turns out to be a fake, I'll want to know how she knew that Mavis Spitforce had departed this world at midnight on Halloween. She has to be high up on the suspect list, along with Marmite Sprat.'

Tilly was delighted to be included in the Friday visit and, while Hettie filled her catnip pipe, she collected the empty plates and poured milk into their cocoa mugs, humming to herself as she went and excited at the prospect of another case for the No. 2 Feline Detective Agency.

'There is just one thing I thought of,' she said, returning to the fireside with the cocoa. 'Who's paying us to sort all this out?'

Hettie brought her smoke ring session to an abrupt halt, coughing and spluttering. Tilly had a point: who was going to pay them? Teezle Makepeace had sought them out after discovering the body, but she had no real responsibility to Mavis Spitforce, and from what they had heard about the dead cat's family, there was no love or money there.

'What a bloody nightmare! The best case we've had for ages and no one to pay the bill, not even expenses. Maybe the friendship club will have a whip round? Miss Spitforce was obviously well in there.'

Tilly looked doubtful. 'Perhaps we could ask Crimola to see if Miss Spitforce would be happy to stump up for us herself?' she suggested, before draining her cocoa mug and pulling her blankets around her. In seconds she was asleep, but Hettie sat long into the night, mulling over the day's events and determined – money or not – to find the cat responsible for the tears she had shed at Whisker Terrace.

CHAPTER SIX

The money came by first post the following morning, a little later than usual and from a very unexpected donor. Both cats had woken early, and Tilly crawled out of her blanket to add some kindling to the fire, coaxing it back to life. She pulled the curtain open slightly and noticed that it was still dark, but the frost had been a hard one and the window looking out over the Butters' backyard was iced in beautiful patterns.

'Jack Frost has been busy,' she said brightly, rinsing the dirty cocoa mugs ready for their morning tea. 'I hope Bruiser is OK in the shed.'

Hettie rubbed her eyes and sat up. 'I'm sure he'll

be fine. He was very pleased to have some shelter, and he'd demolished our dinner before turning in for the night. I bet he got more sleep than I did.' She accepted her tea gratefully, wrapping her paws round it to feel the heat. 'We've got a difficult day ahead of us. I suppose we should see the sister first, although I'd rather have a better look round Miss Spitforce's before the relatives start turning up.'

'Let's go now then,' said Tilly enthusiastically. 'It's very early and we could grab anything interesting and bring it back here before anyone else gets a chance. We could take my tartan shopper.'

The thought of getting up at this time and venturing out into the cold winter's morning held no joy whatsoever for Hettie, but she had to admit that it was a very good idea. 'You're right – we could get all the crime scene stuff out of the way. I'm keen to take a look at anything Miss Spitforce was working on. This book that Irene Peggledrip mentioned and that family history hobby she had – I wonder if she ruffled some feathers there?'

Tilly downed her tea and leapt into action, choosing her warmest cardigan and socks. Hettie struggled from the comfort of her armchair and pulled on yesterday's clothes, which still smelt faintly of paraffin. They banked the fire up, equipped themselves with a torch each, put on their business macs, turned up their collars and stepped out into the hallway to be confronted by

Betty and Beryl Butter hauling the first batch of rustic sticks from the oven.

'Whatever's up?' asked Betty, fighting off a hot flush. 'We're not used to seeing you two about at this time.'

'We have an early house search to do,' Hettie replied, trying to sound important.

'Well, won't the house still be there later?' Beryl forced a tray of bridge rolls into the empty oven. 'Stay there,' she ordered. 'I'll be back in a tick.' She disappeared into the back of the shop and returned minutes later brandishing one of the rustic sticks filled with ham. 'That should sort the pair of you out. Our old mother used to say that leaving the house without breakfast makes a cat repent all day.' Betty nodded in agreement at her sister's borrowed wisdom and placed the food in Tilly's tartan shopper. Delighted with their unexpected breakfast, Hettie and Tilly set off for Whisker Terrace, long before most of the townsfolk were awake.

It was a rare thing to see the Dosh Stores in darkness, and there were no lights on in the rest of the terrace either. Hettie unlocked the door to Miss Spitforce's kitchen, pleased to be getting on with the investigation without the prying eyes of the community. She moved to the window to pull the blind down and shone her torch round the room, relieved to see that everything was how she had left it the night before. The dagger lay with the discarded tea towel on the table; the orange silk shroud and witch's hat were in a heap on the floor; and she hoped that Mavis Spitforce had remained similarly static since she last saw her.

'I think we should make sure that all the blinds and curtains are closed before we start work,' she said. 'We don't want anyone seeing a light and disturbing us. You take the rooms upstairs and I'll do down here.'

Tilly followed Hettie into the parlour, where Miss Spitforce appeared to have spent a peaceful night. The room was icy cold, as if the corpse preferred it that way. Tilly shivered and looked for the door to the stairs, eventually finding it behind a faded velvet curtain. She clambered up the steps, torch in paw, and was faced with a choice of three doors off the small landing: the first opened onto a bathroom; the second onto a bedroom with no bed, but packed instead with boxes, suitcases and old newspapers. Tilly crossed the room to the window which overlooked the front of the terrace, and noticed that there was now a light on at the Dosh Stores; carefully, she pulled the curtains before shining her torch more closely across the contents of the room. Leaving the box room, she opened the final door and found a comfortable looking bedroom. She padded across the pink carpet to the window and saw that this room looked out onto the back garden. It was beginning to get light, but she pulled the curtains and did a circuit of the room with her torch, picking out the bed, a kidney-shaped dressing table, a basket chair and a bedside table piled high with books. Everything was tidy and in its place, including a jewellery box on the dressing table, full of what looked to be valuable trinkets. Tilly closed the box and went back downstairs, avoiding eye contact with Miss Spitforce as she passed through the parlour to the kitchen, where Hettie was slicing the rustic ham stick.

'Everything all right up there?' she asked, licking butter from her paws.

Tilly nodded and took a large bite of the roll that Hettie offered her. Through a mouthful of bread and ham, she revealed her findings. 'There's a box room full of stuff that we might need to have a look at. Her bedroom's tidy. The bed's made and there are some nice bits of jewellery in a box on the dressing table, so I think we can rule out burglars.'

'I suppose it depends on what they were after,' said Hettie, pouring two large mugs of tea from Miss Spitforce's willow pattern teapot. 'I keep remembering what Teezle said about her tracing family histories. What if she found out something terrible? Something so terrible that she had to be silenced for it?'

'Mm – that happens a lot in Agatha Crispy's books. Do you think Miss Spitforce has sugar? That tea pot has made my drink a bit too strong.' Tilly opened several cupboard doors in the kitchen before returning to the table with a box of sugar lumps. 'Is this the dagger she was killed with?'

Hettie nodded. 'Yes. It's not your average kitchen knife, is it? Nasty curled blade and a posh sort of handle – this could be the biggest clue we've got so far. The question is, did the killer bring it or did it belong to Miss Spitforce in the first place?'

Tilly shuddered as she noticed the staining on the blade. 'Shall we stick it in the shopper? I could wrap it in the tea towel to make it safe.'

'That's a good idea. We can show it to Bruiser – he's a mine of information on weapons and that sort of stuff, and he used to pick up odd things like this on his travels. I think we'd better start sorting through papers and anything that might point to a motive. I'll start in the parlour – there's a desk in there. You take the box room.' Tilly was relieved not to have to spend too much time in the company of the late Miss Spitforce. Refreshed from her early breakfast, she bounded up the stairs to start work.

Hettie – having made herself very much at home in Mavis Spitforce's kitchen – reluctantly moved through to the parlour with Tilly's tartan shopper, ready to collect bits and pieces from a puzzle that might or might not lead to the killer. The torch was no good for this job, so she decided to risk switching the desk lamp on, judging that the curtains were thick enough to hide the tell-tale light. She looked at the clock on the mantelpiece; it was already quarter past six, and there was no time to waste. First into the shopper was the pot in which she had hurriedly placed the paper fragments from the dead cat's mouth – an important clue, even if it was unpleasant; whoever had forced Mavis Spitforce to eat someone else's words was obviously making a point.

Then she turned back to the body. As she would have expected, it hadn't moved – but Hettie noticed that it was changing colour, becoming somehow translucent and empty. She thought back to what Irene Peggledrip had said about Miss Spitforce not being there any more, and understood exactly what she meant: the bright, talkative, elderly cat that she had shared tea with several weeks ago had indeed gone, leaving behind no more than a husk in her own image.

Quietly, Hettie set to work on the desk drawers, trying not to disturb the perfect order of bank books, statements and other financial papers. It occurred to her that Mavis had been quite a rich cat, and she wondered who in the family would benefit from her death – if, indeed, she had left her wealth to them in the first place. The question was answered by the third drawer down. Inside, there was a tin box full of sovereigns, a coin that Hettie had only encountered in the town's museum; underneath it was a long document, folded and tied with blue ribbon. She untied the ribbon, guessing that this was the last will and testament of Mavis Spitforce. At a glance, she could see that there was a list of beneficiaries, with several small bequests to friends. Delirium Treemints, she noted, was to inherit the willow pattern tea set, having no doubt acquired quite a reputation for the dispensing of beverages, despite her unsteady paws. Balti Dosh was promised an entire collection of true crime books to feed her thirst for all things morbid, and the rest of the books were to go to Turner Page for the new library, soon to be opened at Furcross House.

Hettie continued to read through the list of names, hoping that something or someone would leap out at her, but there was nothing – nothing, that is, until the final page. The main beneficiaries were both called Spitforce – Mildred and Lavinia. Mildred was now the owner of the tin of sovereigns, and Lavinia had been left a sizeable sum of cash which was to be used to buy a house. So that was the sister and niece accounted for, but it still didn't explain what instructions Mavis had left for her own home in Whisker Terrace. Hettie turned to an attachment clipped to the final page, and there was her answer.

The codicil was dated 20th October, just twelve days ago. Hettie took in the details, and her gasp of surprise coincided with an almighty crash from above which continued down the stairs. Tilly made an ungainly entrance into the parlour, pursued by a number of out-of-control cardboard tubes; she sat dazed for a moment in the middle of Miss Spitforce's hearth rug, rubbing her arthritic paws, but rallied quickly on coming face-to-face with the cold dead eyes that stared out at her from the chaise longue.

Hettie abandoned the will and helped her friend into the kitchen, which was considerably more cheerful than the parlour. She was keen to share her recent revelation, but made sure first that Tilly hadn't suffered any lasting damage. Thankful for the knitted tea cosy that had kept the tea hot, Hettie poured two very strong mugs of it, putting a sugar lump in each and adding an extra one to Tilly's to account for the shock. The milk from the fridge was in short supply, but Miss Spitforce could hardly be blamed for that; the biscuit tin, however, was full and Hettie selected a pawful of chocolate fingers, hoping that they might cheer both Tilly and the tea up a little.

'There's been a breakthrough in our investigation,' she began as Tilly sucked on a chocolate finger soaked in tea. 'I found the will, and guess who gets most of the money and the house?'

'The sister or the niece,' Tilly said, going for the obvious. She knew she was wrong, but she wanted to give Hettie the joy of surprise.

'No, not a bit of it,' Hettie said triumphantly. 'Miss Spitforce added a bequest a couple of weeks ago leaving a small fortune and her house to Irene Peggledrip!'

Tilly missed her mouth with the final chocolate

finger, nearly poking herself in the eye with it. 'Well, that really *is* a breakthrough. Where do we go from here?'

Hettie thought for a moment. 'I think we should stick to our plan of taking anything interesting away with us. I'll have to leave the will and all her private papers here so that the relatives can sort it out when they take over. I don't suppose they'll be too pleased about the Peggledrip windfall, but if you make a quick note of the details in the will before I put it back in the drawer we shouldn't need to see it again. Did you find anything in the box room?'

'Suitcases full of old photos, a chest of clothes, piles of newspapers and a couple of interesting things that we might want to take away with us.'

Hettie waited for her friend to continue, but Tilly was rubbing her head as the after-effects of her fall caught up with her.

'I think we should gather up as much as we can and get you home,' Hettie said, concerned. 'Do we need to take those cardboard tubes with us?'

Tilly nodded. 'Yes, and there's a scrapbook still up there, full of newspaper cuttings. I opened one of the tubes. It was a family history chart, so I think we need to take all of them for a closer look.'

Hettie suddenly remembered something that Teezle Makepeace had said and started lifting the cushions on the kitchen chairs. 'No, there's nothing under them.

I wondered if that chart she hid from Teezle was still there. Anything under your cushion?'

'No, nothing,' Tilly said, leaving chocolate paw prints everywhere. She sat nursing her headache with one paw and noting down the details of Mavis Spitforce's will with the other, while Hettie scurried round collecting as much material as the tartan shopper would allow. She tidied the kitchen, scooping the Halloween trappings off the floor and adding them to the already over-burdened trolley. Satisfied that the house was ready for the relatives to take over, the two cats and the tartan shopper made their way out into the winter's morning, heading home just as the town came to life.

CHAPTER SEVEN

It was a rare thing to see Lavender Stamp delivering the mail. The queen of the High Street Post Office rarely emerged from behind her counter, running her business with an iron claw and making it clear to all who engaged with her that nonsense of any sort would not be tolerated. Her customers feared her; her few friends endured her; and the cats that worked for her lasted as long as her temper would allow. Now, Lavender looked down her bespectacled nose as Hettie and Tilly approached. Admittedly, they looked suspicious, especially at such an early hour: the tartan shopper – already overloaded with what Tilly liked to call 'tangible evidence', a phrase gleaned from one of her books – now bore the extra burden of Tilly herself. Her fall had left her achy and slow, so Hettie had hauled her up onto the top of the shopper, hoping to speed up their progress.

The pavement proved tricky in some places, and there was a bit of a spill outside Hambone's when the cardboard tubes escaped into the gutter, but now, with home in sight, even Tilly had cheered up and was experiencing a fit of the giggles when Lavender Stamp loomed into view.

'Miss Bagshot,' began the postmistress ominously, 'my wretched girl hasn't turned up for work this morning, and as you are . . . er . . . out and about, shall we say, would you be kind enough to take the Butters' letters to them?' She reached into the post bag for a bundle of letters secured with an elastic band and shoved them into Hettie's chest. 'Oh, and before you go I have a parcel for you.' This was said in a rather grudging fashion, as Lavender had never really approved of Hettie and her 'escapades'; equally, it had to be said that Hettie had never really approved of Lavender Stamp, either, and both cats cherished the mutual indifference. Tilly took charge of the parcel and Hettie forced the bundle of letters into her mac pocket as Lavender stalked off down the High Street with her first delivery of the day, more aggressive than usual and looking forward to ringing Teezle Makepeace's neck when she finally turned up for work.

Back in their room, a cheery blaze awaited them as if the fire knew the precise time of their arrival home. Hettie unloaded the contents of the shopper onto the table and Tilly limped to her blanket by the fire, hoping that some heat would ease the growing pain in her limbs.

'I think we'll have to set you up in my armchair for the day,' Hettie said. 'If you're up to it, I need you to go through some of this stuff,' she nodded towards the pile of things on the table. 'You should stay at home in the warm until you feel better. I'll have to go and see Miss Spitforce's sister. I can't put that off any longer – she needs to know, and there's a funeral to arrange.' Hettie crossed to her armchair, plumped up her cushion and lifted Tilly's blanket from the floor. 'Come on. You'll be much more comfortable up here.'

Tilly didn't need to be asked twice, and settled herself in. The heat was getting through to her old bones and she was actually feeling much better, but it was a rare treat to sit in Hettie's chair and she was going to milk it for all it was worth.

Hettie glanced at the parcel that Lavender Stamp had so ungraciously handed over. 'I wonder what this is? I don't remember ordering anything. It's a local postmark. Shall we open it as a treat later?'

Tilly nodded. 'Why do you think Teezle didn't turn up for work? She seemed fine when she left here last night.'

'I got the impression that she was putting a brave

face on it. She'd had quite a shock, finding Miss Spitforce like that. She seems like a good sort who cares about the cats she delivers to – I bet she woke up this morning and just couldn't handle another day at the coalface.'

Tilly was still giggling at the idea of Lavender Stamp with a miner's pick in hand when there was a polite knock at their door. Hettie moved to open it as Bruiser let himself in.

'Mornin' all! Just popped in to see if yer fancy a bite to eat? I'm in the market for a couple of yer landlady's sausage rolls. Can I get yer anything?'

Normally, Hettie would have bitten his paw off for a free breakfast but there were things to be done. 'No time this morning, but you can treat us to dinner later if you like. Wednesday is chicken pie day on the Butters' specials board, and Beryl's cream horns are Tilly's favourite.'

'Right o,' said Bruiser, slightly stung by Hettie's quick response to his half-hearted offer of a sausage roll.

Hettie laughed. 'I was only joking. We get dinner thrown in with our rent so you'll just have to stump up for your own, but you're welcome to eat with us later.'

Bruiser breathed a sigh of relief, knowing that his financial situation was not as healthy as he would like. 'I'll 'ave to get meself a bit of work if I'm stayin' around. If yer hear of anything goin', I'd be pleased to know about it.'

Hettie thought for a moment as she added more coal to the fire. Glancing across at Tilly, she noticed that her friend was fast asleep. She suddenly had an idea and looked up at Bruiser who was standing awkwardly in the open doorway. 'You used to have a motorbike when you lived on the allotments, didn't you?'

Bruiser's scarred old face lit up at the memory. 'Those were the days! My old bike and me doin' a ton on that road to Much-Purrin'. I came off a few times but I 'ad me leathers then, saved me from all sorts.'

Hettie knew that Bruiser would go on for some time about his biker days if she let him, so she brought his raptures to an abrupt end. 'Can you still handle a motorbike? Because if you can, I might be able to offer you a bit of work. There's not much money in it, but enough to buy a dinner or two.'

'Sounds just the job,' said Bruiser, straightening himself up and trying to look respectable enough to re-enter the world of employment. 'All I needs is a dinner and a place that's warm and dry to lay me bones down at the end of a day, and that shed of yours is as cosy as toast. Where's the motorbike, and what do yer want deliverin'?'

Hettie laughed. 'Me, that's what – to all the places I need to go while I'm working on the new case we've just started. As for the motorbike, she's called Scarlet and she lives in Hambone's yard at the moment until I can learn to ride her properly – although I do prefer the sidecar.'

'Sidecar?' said Bruiser, shrinking back in horror. 'She's got a sidecar? That's a real girlie cat thing – not proper bikin' at all.'

The word 'sidecar' had woken Tilly from her nap. She sneezed twice and looked across at Hettie. 'Ooh, I must have nodded off.' She smiled at Bruiser, who saluted her from the door. 'I'm sure someone was shouting about sidecars in my dream. I hope Scarlet is all right. We haven't been for a ride in her this week. Poor Lazarus!'

Bruiser was looking a little confused and Hettie had no time to spare for long explanations. 'Bruiser has agreed to help us today, so I've asked him to drive me about in Scarlet. You can come out with us tomorrow when you're feeling better. You've got to sort through this stuff today.' Hettie pointed to the mountain of papers and tubes on the table.

Tilly looked disappointed at missing out on a spin in Scarlet, but saw the sense in what Hettie was saying. 'I'll get on with it, then – but tell Scarlet that I'll see her tomorrow.'

After calling in to buy two sausage rolls and order their dinner from the Butters, Hettie and Bruiser strode off down the High Street to Hambone's. Meridian waved them through the shop into the backyard, where they were greeted by a mountain of tyres, exhaust pipes and part-built or part-dismantled motorbikes of every sort. As they made their way to the small sales cabin in the far corner of the yard, Bruiser purred with delight at the vision of so many bits of fashioned metal. Lazarus Hambone took up most of the space in the cabin. He was a giant of a cat and the fact that one of his hind legs was now encased in a plaster cast made things extremely difficult. He was resting it on the open bottom drawer of his filing cabinet, which made it impossible for anyone else to fit into the office space.

Hettie stood in the doorway to introduce Bruiser. 'Sorry to hear about your accident. I have a difficult case on at the moment, and I wondered if I could use Scarlet? My friend Bruiser here has offered to take me out on her.'

Lazarus put down the *Biker Monthly* he was reading and – still seated – reached for a set of keys from the board above his desk. 'It's about time you managed the wheels yerself instead of sittin' in the sidecar with yer friend. Where is she today? It's not like her to miss a ride out.'

Hettie took the keys from Lazarus's giant paw. 'She had to do some work in the office today, but she hopes your leg will mend soon. Is Scarlet parked in her usual place?'

Lazarus nodded, looking Bruiser up and down. 'She

needs a good strong kick to start 'er up, but once you give 'er a bit o' throttle she'll fly. You got any leathers? Not the weather to go without.'

Bruiser admitted that he hadn't expected to be working for Hettie and had shed his leathers some years ago. Lazarus pointed to the back of his cabin door. 'Take that jacket. A customer left it months ago and he's not been back for it. That should keep the wind out. There's a helmet on the floor down there. You can 'ave the jacket but the helmet'll 'ave to be a borrow as it belongs to me old ma.'

Bruiser offered his thanks and eagerly pulled on the leather jacket, which was a perfect fit. Grabbing the helmet from the cabin floor, he crossed the yard to where Hettie was standing next to a bright red motorbike and sidecar. His eyes lit up. 'Cor blimey! What a beauty! I take it all back – nothing girlie about her. She's a goddess on three wheels. I can't wait ter get her fired up.'

Hettie was pleased at Bruiser's enthusiasm. She pulled back the lid to the sidecar and clambered in. 'We'd better get going. You'll have to wheel her through the double gates at the back of the yard.'

Bruiser took charge of the bike and guided it out through the gates onto the road. 'Where're we goin' first?'

'Cheapcuts Lane. There are some flats at the bottom, and we have to call at number seven.' Hettie closed the lid on the sidecar, settling herself down in the plush comfort of Tilly's homemade cushions and pulling the tartan travel rug around her. Bruiser crammed Meridian Hambone's helmet on his head, kicked Scarlet into life, and sped off.

The journey in Scarlet was exhilarating, although Hettie almost revisited her rustic ham stick on the roundabout at the bottom of Sheba Gardens. Bruiser had enjoyed his first circuit so much that he repeated the manoeuvre three times before taking the exit road that would bring them in at Cheapcuts Lane. The small flats at the bottom of the road looked cold and unwelcoming, and this part of the town was to be avoided unless you enjoyed fighting or similar anti-social behaviour. It wasn't so much that the residents were poor; it was more a case of their refusing to comply with rules that had been laid down by others; they were perfectly happy with the way things were, and had collectively decided to rail against anyone whose agenda was to make the world a better place.

Bruiser brought the bike to a shuddering standstill outside the flats, attracting immediate attention from a legion of kittens that appeared from nowhere and proceeded to bounce up and down on the roof of the sidecar, much to Hettie's dismay. Bruiser rose to the occasion by offering his fiercest hiss and spit routine, which held the hordes at bay long enough for Hettie to clamber out onto the pavement. Looking round, she tightened the belt on her mac as if preparing for battle. 'I think you should stay with the bike in case this lot get any ideas about borrowing her.'

'Right-o,' said Bruiser, pleased not to be parted from his new toy. 'Any bother, though, and you just gives me a shout. I was brought up near here, and I know how it all works. Yer gives as good as yer gets, and yer gotta earn respect – that's the way of it.'

Hettie was grateful for the advice but felt rather overdressed in her smart designer mac. She knew that the information she was about to deliver would not endear her in any way to this area of the town, but the sooner it was done, the better her chances of catching the killer who was still at large.

The door to number 7 was scratched and grimy; the paint had peeled some time ago and the letterbox was just a hole in the door; there were no trimmings and no pride, just a way of getting in and out of what looked to be little more than a box connected to other boxes. There was no bell or knocker, either, so Hettie thumped on the door as politely as she could and waited.

It was some time before she heard a shuffling from inside, followed by the appearance of two eyes looking through the letterbox hole. Hettie bent down to show herself in the hope that the door would eventually be opened.

'I don't want anything you got, so clear off!' said

the letterbox that had now turned into a mouth.

Hettie stood back and shouted at the door. 'I need to speak with Miss Mildred Spitforce. Is she at home? I have some distressing news for her.'

The eyes returned to the letterbox and then the mouth again. 'Maybe she is or maybe she isn't, and who might you be?'

'I'm Hettie Bagshot of the No. 2 Feline Detective Agency, and I must speak with Miss Spitforce urgently. Can you help?'

Hettie was tiring of her conversation with the door and was just about to scribble a note to stick through the letterbox when she heard the sound of bolts being drawn across. The door resisted to start with, but eventually swung back to reveal a thin and feeble version of Mavis Spitforce, and Hettie wasted no time in delivering her message. 'Ah, I can see that you are Mildred Spitforce and I'm afraid I have some bad news. Your sister Mavis is dead.'

Hettie was hoping that she might be invited into the flat to discuss the finer points of Mavis's death with her sister in private, but no invitation was forthcoming. Instead, Mildred Spitforce threw back her head and laughed. 'Bad news, you say? Why, it's the best news I've had in years. Miss High and Mighty gone for good? Now that really *is* a cause for celebration.'

Hettie had been warned by Teezle Makepeace that there was no love lost between the sisters, but she hadn't expected her news to bring such joy and she was keen to wipe the smile from Mildred's face. 'I think you should know that your sister was murdered, and I am at present investigating who might have done that.'

'Murder, you say? Seems like someone got to her before I did. She had it coming to her, that's for sure, with all her meddling and her thinking she was better than the rest of us and her delving into things that didn't concern her.'

Hettie could feel eyes trained on her from everywhere around the flats: doors had been half opened, and one or two cats had come out on the pretence of sweeping their doorsteps.

'Do you think I could step inside for a moment, Miss Spitforce? I'd be grateful if you could tell me a little more about your sister.'

Mildred could see that her neighbours were homing in on her visitor and their conversation, and reluctantly ushered Hettie into her front room, nodding grudgingly to a chair. 'Sit down if you want to. There's no heat till later so you may as well keep your coat on. What do you want to know?'

Hettie doubted that the front room had ever had any heat, and instantly noticed the drop in temperature when she stepped in from outside. The room was a sad reflection of a life lived without colour or hope: no cheerful trappings, no photographs, just plain and sparse – a far cry from Mavis Spitforce's comfortable home.

'You seem to think that your sister deserved to be killed – is there any particular reason why?'

Mildred Spitforce laughed again. 'Why, you say? I'll tell you why! She broke my heart, that's what she did – took away the only thing I ever loved.' A deep sob came from somewhere inside Mildred Spitforce and her frail body seemed wracked with the pain of her loss.

Hettie sat and waited for the waters to calm a little before responding. 'May I ask what it was that your sister took from you?'

'My girl, Livvy. She was just a kitten and she snatched her away, said I couldn't look after her properly, filled her head full of books. Spoilt her, she did – just like Merry Spitforce did with her when we were growing up. He never had time for me once Ma had gone.'

Hettie began to understand what had driven the sisters apart, but she was still confused. 'You mentioned Merry Spitforce – who is he?'

'He's my old dad, gone now and good riddance. Left all his money to Mavis, he did, because she looked after him. They were always sharing secrets. When Livvy got older, she shared secrets with Mavis. Neither of them ever shared any secrets with me.'

'What sort of secrets?' asked Hettie.

'How the hell should I know? They were secrets.'

'Where is Lavinia now?'

'She lives out Much-Purring way, lodges with Bugs Anderton and teaches at the village school. I never see her. She's far too grand to call on me.'

Hettie was beginning to feel sorry for Mildred Spitforce, despite her indifference to Mavis's death, but there were things that had to be done and Mavis could not lie indefinitely in her parlour. 'Your sister's body is still in her house at Whisker Terrace. Is there anyone who will take responsibility for the . . . er . . . arrangements?'

Mildred had recovered a little and returned to her earlier bravado. 'Well, that's nothing to do with me, although I wouldn't mind having a look at her now that she can't have a go at me. Hang on a minute – I'll get my coat.'

Mildred had taken Hettie by surprise; the last thing she had expected was to be ferrying her across town to view her sister's corpse, but that's exactly what appeared to be happening. The motorbike and sidecar were not where she had left them, but no sooner had she sworn under her breath than Scarlet roared into view, Bruiser giving her full throttle to the delight of at least half a dozen kittens who had crammed themselves into the sidecar for a free ride.

The kittens tumbled out as Bruiser applied the brakes. Hettie did her best to help Mildred into the sidecar, then closed the lid to avoid any further conversation and clambered up behind Bruiser. 'Do you know Whisker Terrace?' she shouted above the din of the bike's engine. Bruiser nodded and spun the machine around. They travelled back up Cheapcuts Lane, past Jessie's shop and out onto the High Street, narrowly missing Lavender Stamp who was on her second postal round of the day.

There was quite a crowd in Whisker Terrace as Bruiser swung the motorbike round the corner. Balti Dosh was deep in conversation with Hacky Redtop from the local paper, and his sidekick Prunella Snap was taking pictures of the crowd that had gathered outside Mavis Spitforce's front door. Bruiser parked the bike outside the Dosh Stores, and Hettie groaned at the sight of so many sightseers.

'Bloody marvellous!' she said. 'How are we going to get in there without being noticed? We'll be mobbed, and Hacky Redtop won't let it drop until he's got a story.'

'Come on,' said Bruiser, helping Mildred out of the sidecar. 'There's an alleyway round the back that leads to the gardens. We've just got to work out which house is which.'

Mildred responded immediately. 'I know the one. Mavis didn't like me coming to the front door, so I always went round the back.' Mildred led the way past the Dosh Stores and round the corner into the alleyway. A high wall ran down both sides, punctuated every so often by a tall garden gate. Mildred chose the second gate, but it was bolted and Bruiser sprang into action, bounding over the wall and opening the gate from the inside to let Hettie and Mildred into the garden.

'I'll stand guard by the gate while you go in, just in case we get any trouble at the back.'

Hettie had quite forgotten how decisive Bruiser was and welcomed his protective qualities. He was certainly earning his bed and board. She felt for the key in her mac pocket and steered Mildred Spitforce up the garden towards the house. 'Are you sure you want to do this? She's been dead for some time.'

Mildred nodded and Hettie forced the key into the lock, opening the door into the kitchen. Once inside, she locked the door behind them in case the gathering crowd at the front decided to try their luck.

'She's in the parlour. Would you like me to come with you?'

Mildred looked nervous, as if the news of her sister's death was finally registering. 'I've never seen anyone dead before. I ran away when Ma died. They laid her out in her coffin for people to visit, but I couldn't look.'

Hettie was beginning to wish that she had been successful in closing Mavis Spitforce's eyes before allowing her family to view the corpse, but nothing could be done now. 'You could wait until the undertakers have made her more . . . er . . . comfortable,' she suggested as Mildred moved towards the parlour, but it was she who was actually more shocked by what confronted them: Mavis Spitforce's body was gone, and all that remained was the blanket that Hettie had thrown over her.

'I don't understand,' said Hettie, speaking out loud. 'She was here a couple of hours ago.'

'Perhaps she wasn't dead,' offered Mildred, slumping down on the chaise longue which her sister had so recently vacated. 'It's just like her to perform a miracle to disappoint me.'

'That's not possible. She was really very dead and certainly not capable of going anywhere under her own steam.' Hettie looked round the room, sensing that there were other things out of place as well as the missing corpse. Her attention was drawn to the desk and one of the drawers which was slightly open; the clock on the mantelpiece was no longer in its central position; and the door that led through to the short hallway was wide open. Hettie could see the front door, which she hadn't been aware of before.

Mildred shivered. 'Good to know she scrimped on her heating as well. It's freezing in here.'

Suddenly there was a sound from above as if a door was being closed. Mildred and Hettie both looked towards the stairs as the rhythmic beat of footsteps came closer to the parlour. The two cats braced themselves, preparing to see the ghost of Mavis Spitforce appear from behind the stair curtain; afterwards, it was hard to decide if they were disappointed or relieved when reality spoke.

'Well, I didn't think it would be long before the family vulture turned up.' The comment was addressed directly towards Mildred Spitforce, and it was clear to Hettie that the cat who joined them in the parlour was her daughter, Lavinia. 'And I see you've brought a friend with you to help carry off the spoils. Well, it won't surprise you to learn that she left you absolutely nothing, so you can get out of my house right now.'

Hettie looked at the dejected form of Mildred Spitforce, considered the spiteful nature of Lavinia's words, and couldn't resist wading in. 'That's not entirely true, Miss Spitforce. Your aunt left a box of sovereigns to your mother. You are correct in assuming that you are a beneficiary, but I regret to inform you that this is *not* your house.'

Lavinia Spitforce looked first at Hettie and then at Mildred before adopting her school teacher's voice. 'I'm not interested in anything you have to say. I know what has been promised to me, and whatever you have dreamt up between you is incorrect. Now, if you would be kind enough to leave, I will get on with the business of organising a funeral.'

Mildred Spitforce stood and turned on her daughter.

'You wicked little madam! Where is the grief? Where are the tears? And where is my sister?'

Lavinia sneered, showing perfect teeth. 'It's a bit late for all this, isn't it? Suddenly caring now she's dead. She was old. Old cats die. *You'll* die soon. There's no time for grief – we're born, we make our own way, and then we die. I've had her taken away. I don't want her cluttering the place up while I sort through her rubbish. If you're desperate to see her, she'll be tucked up at Shroud and Trestle's – they carted her off half an hour ago. She got a great send-off from her neighbours. They're still out there now.'

Hettie shook her head in disgust, remembering the pride with which Mavis Spitforce had spoken of her niece during their tea time chats. She decided to try and take control of the situation before Lavinia destroyed her mother completely. 'Miss Spitforce, you refer to your aunt's death as a natural progression of life, but I should point out to you that her death was by no means natural. Someone chose to plunge a knife into her back and then dress her up as a pumpkin while she was seated at her kitchen table.' She enjoyed the look of horror on Lavinia's face; Mildred appeared to have gone into shock, and at last mother and daughter seemed to have found some common ground. Lavinia opened her mouth to speak, but Hettie pressed on. 'Your aunt was murdered, this house is a crime scene, and – whatever your expectations were – your aunt drew up a new will a couple of weeks ago, and this house has been left to someone else.'

'Oh, you mean this worthless bit of paper?' sneered Lavinia, pulling the will from her coat pocket. She reached behind her and took a box of matches off the mantelpiece, then threw the will into the empty grate and lit it before Hettie could react. 'There you are!' she continued. 'The old will still stands, and in that one I get everything.' The angry cat crossed to the desk and yanked the third drawer open with some force, then took the box of sovereigns out and threw it across the room at her mother. 'Here, take what she left you and go. That's all you're getting. If you've a fancy for anything else, you'll have to buy it from a charity shop. I'm getting the house cleared tomorrow, and anyway, none of this stuff would fit in that nasty little box you call home.'

The coins broke loose from the tin and Hettie gathered them together while Mildred's sobs shook the chaise longue. There was a piece of paper in the bottom of the box, and a quick glance told Hettie that it was a letter from Mavis to Mildred; she replaced the coins and pocketed the letter to look at later, just in case it shed further light on the sisters' relationship. Now, there were some unanswered questions regarding Lavinia Spitforce and Hettie took what she knew might be her last chance to confront her. 'Before we go, Miss Spitforce, I should inform you that my colleagues and I are investigating the circumstances surrounding your aunt's murder. I wonder if I might ask you a couple of questions?'

Lavinia laughed. 'Oh, how exciting! Am I the number one suspect? I think you should know a little more about my aunt before you draw your conclusions. You might want to extend the list of cats who'll be pleased to be rid of her.'

Hettie avoided a passionate desire to slap Lavinia's face and grabbed the opportunity offered. 'As you point out, I *didn't* know Mavis Spitforce very well. Perhaps you could tell me what she was like?'

Lavinia took the bait and rose to the occasion. 'Well, let me see, three words should do it: controlling, overbearing and manipulative – that about sums her up.' She gestured towards her mother. 'Now, perhaps you'd leave me alone and take her with you.'

Hettie helped Mildred to her feet while Lavinia began taking pictures off the wall and stacking them on the floor as if her visitors had left already. 'Just one more question before we go,' she said, determined to fire a parting shot. 'How did you know your aunt had died?'

'What do you mean, how?' asked Lavinia, playing for time. 'Everyone knows. But as a matter of fact, my landlady told me.'

'Miss Anderton?' Hettie clarified, scoring a point.

Lavinia looked unsettled but spoke out, wanting to

bring the conversation to an end. 'Well, you have been busy. Yes, Bugs Anderton. My aunt sent me to live with her so I'd be close to my job at the school. I won't be living there any more, though – being spied upon, having my things gone through. She's as bad as Aunt Mavis, what with her and her friendship club – all those stupid sad cats gathered together once a week to hear talks by boring cats on boring subjects. It's pathetic, really.'

Hettie gathered up Mildred and the box of sovereigns and made her way to the back door, unlocking it and inadvertently sliding the key into her pocket before Lavinia could notice. She was pleased to see Bruiser still guarding the back gate, and the three cats made their way round to the Dosh Stores where Bruiser helped Mildred into the sidecar and clambered onto the motorbike. Hettie was about to join him when her arm was nearly tugged out of its socket by a very enthusiastic Balti Dosh.

'Oh Miss Bagshot, whatever can be happening? We saw them come and take Miss Spitforce away. I held the gate open so they could get her through. They say she has been murdered by Milky Myers! Is there blood in her kitchen? Can we go in and look round? It is most exciting!'

By now, the crowd had shifted from Mavis's front door and was gathering round Hettie, hopeful of some lurid details to take home. Hacky Redtop barged through the crowd with his notepad and pencil poised for a statement, just as the local TV crew arrived and started setting up a camera tripod. Prunella Snap seemed to have got into an altercation with one of the TV reporters and had been pushed to the ground, where she became entangled in the microphone cable that was being rolled out by a regional radio engineer. Delirium Treemints had laid out a table of refreshments on the pavement opposite the house and was doing a brisk trade in tea and morning coffee, using the Dosh Stores to boil her kettle. It seemed that Lavinia Spitforce was right about one thing: everyone seemed to know that Mavis Spitforce was dead, even before Shroud and Trestle had taken her away.

Hettie raised her paw and silenced the crowd. 'I can confirm that Miss Mavis Spitforce has died,' she said in her best official tone. 'I am investigating the reasons for this and have nothing further to say at this time. However, I'm sure Miss Spitforce's niece Lavinia will be happy to talk. She is inside the house at the moment, and I suggest that one of you knock on the door and invite her out to speak to you.'

Hettie had hardly finished the sentence before the crowd shifted as one, laying siege once again to Mavis's front door. Bruiser kicked the bike into life as Hettie – treating herself to a satisfied grin – leapt on the back, and Scarlet roared away from the community scrum, leaving an unsuspecting Lavinia Spitforce to the mercy of the hungry media.

Having met her daughter, Hettie reviewed her opinion of Mildred Spitforce and promised to keep her informed of any developments in the case when they dropped her off at her flat. But the most urgent thing on the agenda now was lunch, and Bruiser responded by getting them to the Butters' in a matter of minutes, parking Scarlet outside the post office. Hettie had a fancy for a prawn bap – a new line that Beryl had introduced to the lunchtime specials – and chose a sardine and cream cheese roll for Tilly, while Bruiser settled for a beef pasty. The cats made their way through to the backyard, where Hettie picked the milk up from the doorstep and opened the door on a hive of activity.

The whole of the room was laid out with charts and Tilly was sitting in the middle of them, scribbling notes. She was so engrossed that she didn't realise she had company until the smell of Bruiser's pasty reached her nostrils.

'Oh, lovely!' she exclaimed as Hettie put lunch down on the only corner of the table that wasn't covered by family histories. She rose from her labours and paddled across the sea of papers to the kettle, where she prepared three mugs with her best visitors' tea bags, kept for what she liked to call 'working lunches' – although whenever food was available, work tended to grind to a halt. Hettie and Tilly both believed firmly in getting their priorities right.

'That's a beauty,' said Bruiser, eyeing up the dagger that Hettie had removed so recently from Mavis Spitforce's back. 'Last time I saw one of these was when it whistled past me ear in Billy Smut's circus.'

Hettie proffered the dagger to Bruiser for a closer look. 'What sort is it?'

Bruiser took it and turned it in his paws. 'It's one of them ceremonial jobs, valuable I'd say – look it's got some jewels in the hilt. Nasty curved blade, too – comes from overseas, not yer general sort of dagger. The cat I knew at the circus had a set of 'em for his act. He came from somewhere in the Himalayas. Funny sort of cat, 'e was – in a trance most of the time, and not exactly talkative.'

Bruiser returned the dagger to its tea towel, cleared himself a space at the table and noisily launched himself into his pasty. Tilly sat on her blanket by the fire and sucked the cream cheese out of her roll before setting about the sardines and the bread. Hettie opened her bap and ate the prawns first, then licked the sauce, and finally posted the bread into her mouth just as the kettle came to the boil. Nothing was said as the cats licked and cleaned themselves, and it was Hettie who eventually spoke. 'This is a rum old case. If I hadn't met Mavis Spitforce, I'd have said she had it coming to her. On the face of it, she treated her sister very badly and the niece is one of the most revolting cats I've ever met – yet Mavis thought the sun shone out of her. It just doesn't add up.'

Not wishing to intrude, Bruiser excused himself from agency business and took himself off for an afternoon nap down the shed. Hettie brought Tilly up to speed with the morning's events before settling down with her to look at the charts they'd removed from Mavis Spitforce's box room.

'The most interesting thing I've found so far is this one,' said Tilly, unfolding a large piece of paper which chronicled several generations of one family. 'Look at the name at the top.'

Hettie screwed her eyes up; the print was small and handwritten. 'It looks like Thaddeus something,' she said. 'Why is that interesting?'

Tilly beamed. 'Ah well, the "something" is important. Look halfway down the page.' She pointed with her paw. 'See what that says?'

Hettie tried to make out the name. 'Murry Spil . . . no, it's not Spil, it's S-P-I . . . T. Yes, it's a 'T', but the rest of the name is a squiggle.'

'SPITFORCE!' said Tilly, clapping her paws together with excitement. 'Once you get used to the handwriting you can work it out. And it's Merry, not Murry.'

Hettie looked closer and agreed that it was indeed 'Spitforce'. 'Merry was Mavis's and Mildred's father,' she said. 'So this is *their* family tree?'

'Exactly,' Tilly confirmed, getting even more excited. 'Now go back to the top of the page. You got the

Thaddeus bit right, but look at the second name again.'

Hettie stared at the paper, confused. 'Well, it certainly isn't Spitforce. That's not an 'S' and the name is too short anyway. It looks like an 'M'. Come on, help me out – what does it say?'

'It says "MYERS"! Thaddeus MYERS! And looking at the rest of the family, I'd say that Thaddeus's nickname was MILKY. Look – here are his parents and brother and sister; all of them died on the same day. October 31st – Halloween. But Thaddeus survived. He went on to have a son and his son's son was Merry Spitforce. They must have changed their name along the way. It doesn't say when Thaddeus died, though.'

Hettie stared at the chart. 'So Milky Myers was Mavis's and Mildred's great, great grandfather. That's why Mavis was so cross about Marmite Sprat's book – it was her family that Marmite was writing about.'

Tilly was delighted with her morning's work, especially as Hettie seemed pleased.

'There are a couple of other family charts that Mavis had been working on,' she added, searching through the mountain of paper on the table. 'She didn't get very far with this one.'

Hettie looked at the names. This document was much easier to read, and at the bottom of the page she could clearly make out a whole row of Doshes: Rogan, Balti, Bhaji, Masala, Pakora. To make it more interesting, Mavis had traced the family shops as well. 'That's quite an empire,' she said in admiration. 'The Doshes have stores all over the place. Look – Southwool, Much-Purring, and all the villages in between. She's gone back to Rogan's great grandfather. Looks like a work in progress to me – it's a shame she didn't finish it.'

'She managed to get through several rows of Andertons, though,' Tilly said. 'She's traced her back to The Battle of Flooded Field. I think it says she's got Scottish royalty flowing through her veins – no wonder she's so bossy.'

Hettie thought for a moment as Tilly set about rolling up the charts and putting them back into their tubes. The case was complicated, offering several lines of enquiry and a substantial number of suspects. She added some thinking coal to the fire and slumped down in her armchair, tired and confused. So much had happened in such a short spell of time, but as far as she could see the only real breakthrough was the Milky Myers connection to Mavis Spitforce, and she had no idea where that got them.

Tilly could see the frustration in Hettie's face and knew that the time had come for what she liked to call a 'case review'. Putting the last of the charts in the staff sideboard, she snatched up her notepad and perched on the arm of Hettie's chair. 'Shall we write down a list of suspects?' she asked encouragingly, doing her best to stop Hettie from dozing off.

Hettie sat up, knowing that the job had to be

done. 'Well, I wouldn't trust her family as far as I could throw them, so put Lavinia Spitforce at the top. Mildred can go on the list, too, although I doubt she was involved. We'll have to pay a visit to Bugs Anderton in Much-Purring – she seems to have been close to Mavis and maybe she can shed some light on Lavinia and the change of will. We'll put Bugs on the list for now. Marmite Sprat is a contender, especially as bits of her latest effort were stuffed in Mavis Spitforce's mouth. I'm not sure about Delirium Treemints; I doubt she could aim straight enough to stab anyone in the back, but we could put her down as an outsider along with Balti Dosh and Teezle Makepeace.'

Tilly had dutifully noted down the names until she got to Teezle's. 'Surely you don't think she was involved?'

Hettie looked at the growing list, 'Well, she had the opportunity: she's in and out of those old cats' houses every day and she's the sort that no one notices. She's hooked off work for the day as well, so she could be miles away by now.'

Tilly added Teezle to the list. 'What about Milky Myers? Should I put him down? He'd be about a hundred and fifty by now.'

Hettie laughed. 'There's no harm in sticking him down. A lot of cats on that list seem to think he's done it. Don't forget Irene Peggledrip – she got Mavis's house before dear Lavinia burnt the latest will. I'm looking forward to seeing her on Friday, and if the story of Milky Myers has anything to do with this case at all it will be helpful to have a look round the old house and grounds.'

'What's next?' asked Tilly, eyeing up the clock on the staff sideboard. 'It's ten past two. We could go to Much-Purring for a run out in Scarlet.'

Hettie wondered whether she could handle another conversation with Bugs Anderton so soon after the Methodist Hall gathering, but she knew that time was running out and their list of suspects had to be eliminated one by one. 'OK, that's a good idea – but you can go down the shed and convince Bruiser to forsake his nap and get his leathers on.'

Tilly had quite forgotten her tumble down Mavis Spitforce's stairs and skipped round the room choosing a warm cardigan from the filing cabinet and searching out the woolly hat that she reserved for outings in Scarlet's sidecar. Dressed for the cold November day, she scampered down the garden path in search of Bruiser. Hettie put her business mac back on, banked up the fire and picked up Scarlet's keys. She had a feeling that it was going to be a very long afternoon.

CHAPTER EIGHT

The post office had just reopened after lunch, and Lavender Stamp's queue had begun to form outside. Lavender herself had had no time for lunch, which put her in a particularly bad frame of mind. It was some years since she had relinquished her domain behind the counter to deliver the post on foot, but doing both jobs was almost beyond her. There had been no word from Teezle Makepeace, not even the hint of an excuse, and Lavender had resigned herself to preparing an advertisement for a post-cat which she intended to display in her shop window the following day if no word was received.

There were, however, plenty of words on the piece of official post office stationery that had been glued to Scarlet's sidecar windscreen. After a great deal of scraping and scratching, and a generous amount of spit for the final stages, Hettie released the note from the windscreen. It read:

IN THE INTERESTS OF THE WIDER COMMUNITY, IT WOULD BE ALTOGETHER MORE HELPFUL FOR YOU TO ESTABLISH A PARKING AREA FOR THIS PARTICULAR VEHICLE WHERE IT CAN CAUSE NO OFFENCE OR DISRUPTION TO THE POST OFFICE AND ITS CUSTOMERS.

'I think Lavender Stamp is trying to tell us something,' said Hettie, sliding back the lid on the sidecar and helping Tilly into her seat. Bruiser, pulled from his afternoon nap, crammed the ill-fitting helmet onto his head and leapt onto the bike, giving Hettie very little time to settle herself next to Tilly in the sidecar before he was off down the High Street and heading out of town towards Much-Purring-on-the-Rug.

Hettie and Tilly pulled their travel blanket round them as they watched the town whizz by. Bruiser's face was contorted against the speed of the motorbike and he drove like a cat possessed, only slowing down when absolutely necessary to avoid other vehicles. Had it not been for some quick thinking and an alternative route through a front garden, things could have turned nasty outside the Peggledrip house as Rogan Dosh and his delivery van emerged from Irene's driveway at just the wrong moment.

Out on the open road, though, Scarlet excelled herself and it was only minutes before they entered the village of Much-Purring-on-the-Rug. The realisation that they had absolutely no idea where Bugs Anderton lived dawned on Hettie as Bruiser brought the motorbike to an abrupt standstill in a lay-by outside the ancient village church. Clambering out of the sidecar, Hettie looked for divine intervention; it materialised quite miraculously in the shape of a cloaked and gaitered vicar, who looked older than the church he served.

The elderly cat came forward in a spirit of welcome and introduced himself. 'I am the Reverend Jacob Surplus. May I be of assistance?'

Hettie put on her best posh voice and addressed the vicar. 'That is so very kind of you. I am Hettie Bagshot of the No. 2 Feline Detective Agency, and I am looking for Miss Anderton's house.'

Tilly giggled as Hettie engaged with the apparition from the past. The Reverend Jacob Surplus shrank back as if he'd been burnt with a poker. 'Methodists! Too good for the fires of hell. When the day of judgement comes they shall be drowned in the firmament and the locusts shall come and eat their eyes, and their bodies shall be dissected and thrown to the four winds.'

This was rather more than Hettie had bargained for, but she persisted nonetheless. 'Absolutely, couldn't agree more – but in the meantime, could you point us in the direction of Miss Anderton's house?'

The vicar lifted his paw in the direction of the village. 'Satan's plot, just after the Dosh Stores on the left.' And with that he hobbled away towards the church.

Bruiser elected to stay with the motorbike, and Hettie and Tilly set off to walk into the village. It was very much an old-world scene of thatched cottages, rough gardens with a few dying vegetables, and lines of washing, damp and lifeless in the November gloom. In high summer, Hettie imagined that it was a very different place, with gardens of roses, whitewashed walls and cats chatting congenially over garden gates or sleeping in the sun on their doorsteps. There was to her mind no special season for half-wits, though: they always seemed in plentiful supply in the countryside, fit for nothing but work on the land and courting the wrong branch of the family, which gave rise to the problem in the first place. Much-Purring had a reputation for such cats, but mercifully they never seemed to leave the village, so the problem – if it was a problem – kept itself to itself.

The village green was in sight before they identified the Much-Purring branch of the Dosh Stores, run by Rogan's Aunt Pakora. She had fought a bitter battle with Rogan's father to take over the shop, which had been in the male cat's branch of the family for as long as anyone could remember. Masala Dosh – having lost out to his sister – opened a sea front shop in Southwool and had recently expanded his interests into the 'Loads of Dosh' amusement arcade, making sure that there were plenty of male heirs to follow on from him. Pakora had improved on her empire by purchasing shops in several other villages as and when they became available, giving the family a monopoly in the area between Much-Purring and the sea.

As Hettie and Tilly approached the Stores, Pakora was freshening the vegetable racks outside, selecting one or two items to add to the giant vat of curry that was always simmering on her kitchen stove at the back of the shop. For those in the village who had little interest in cooking, Pakora's curries and home-baked naans were a life saver; she also bought in samosas from Rogan's town shop to beef up her take away service, which had blossomed since she acquired a three-wheeler bicycle with a large boot.

Hettie made the approach. 'Excuse me, I wonder if you could help me?'

Pakora looked up from her carrots. 'I will try. What is your wish?'

'We're looking for Miss Anderton's house.'

Pakora abandoned her carrots and moved out onto the path. 'Miss Anderton lives in that extremely nice house next door to my extremely nice shop. Just there – look,' she pointed a paw full of exotic rings in the direction of a rather plain but perfect new build, set back from the road and bordered by trees and a white picket fence. It occurred to Hettie that if she had had to find the house without help, this was the one she would have chosen; it stood out for its perfect lines and complete lack of character. In the town it would have been very desirable, but amid the old country cottages and terraces it took on a rather 'look at me' quality.

Pakora returned to her vegetables, blowing the dust off some mushrooms, and Hettie and Tilly made their way down Bugs Anderton's perfectly straight concrete path. The door was plain except for the knocker, an elaborate affair polished within an inch of its life and made in the shape of a thistle, a clear nod towards Bugs's ancestors. Hettie raised her paw to the knocker, only to be thwarted by an early response from Bugs herself who opened the door and beamed at her visitors.

'Miss Bagshot! What a lovely surprise, and your friend, too. Welcome, welcome, welcome. Please come in.'

Hettie and Tilly trod carefully on her perfect cream carpet and followed their host down the hall. Bugs ushered them into her sitting room, which – following the trend of the hallway – was also very cream.

Somewhat radically, the sofa and two fireside chairs teetered on beige but the antimacassars were a perfect match with the carpet. The only real flash of colour was Bugs herself: the combination of ginger hair and a duck egg blue trouser suit was very striking indeed, if striking was the right word.

'Please sit down and make yourselves at home. I was about to take my afternoon tea. May I tempt you to a salmon sandwich and a shortbread finger?'

Feeling awkward but not wanting to disappoint, Hettie and Tilly nodded in unison and Bugs glided from the room, leaving them to wonder exactly what they'd got themselves into. Hettie struggled from her mac, laying it across the arm of the sofa, and Tilly responded by removing her woolly hat and undoing the top button of her cardigan. 'It's a bit scary in here,' she said, looking for somewhere to hide her hat so that the rainbow effect wouldn't offend the décor. 'Even the pictures are sepia.'

Hettie studied the framed landscape over the fireplace. It was a harvest scene of cats gathering hay, with mountains in the distance, a small farmhouse, and an old tractor pulling a cart. Hettie marvelled at just how many shades of cream and beige the artist had used to create the painting, and it came as no surprise to her that the work was signed 'B. Anderton'. The alcove next to the fireplace sported a photograph of a rather beautiful old cottage with a thatched roof; in the foreground, an elderly cat in a long dress and mop cap smiled out from the picture.

The arrival of the hostess trolley put an end to Hettie's art appraisal. Unlike most of its kind, this trolley didn't squeak and seemed easy to manoeuvre; like its owner, it sailed across the thick-pile cream carpet as if on air.

'Ah, I see you appreciate a country scene, Miss Bagshot,' said Bugs, parking the trolley next to the sofa. 'I find them so colourful and invigorating – just the thing to cheer us up on these cold winter days. The old cottage you're looking at was here before I had my house built – not at all what I was looking for, so I had it knocked down and utilised the plot to its best advantage.'

Hettie couldn't resist sharing a look with Tilly as Bugs prepared china cups decorated with refreshingly pink rosebuds; the tea plates matched, but it was hard to make a judgement on the teapot as it was swathed in a beige tea cosy embellished with cream embroidery. It occurred to her that the trolley had been prepared in advance as if visitors were expected. The first two tiers of the cake stand were filled with perfectly cut salmon sandwiches, garnished with watercress, and on the bottom there was an array of sugar-dusted shortbread.

Bugs passed the plates round and followed with the cake stand. Tilly took the sandwich closest to her for fear of upsetting the display, and Hettie did the same.

Then came cream serviettes and finally the tea.

'I should tell you, Miss Bagshot, that I was expecting you to call,' said Bugs, replacing her cup on its saucer. 'Lavinia telephoned me and said you were looking into the circumstances of her aunt's death. She was rather upset, and seemed to think that you regarded her as your number one suspect.'

Hettie absent-mindedly reached for another sandwich. 'I'm afraid that everyone is a suspect at this stage in the case. There is a considerable list of cats who might have wanted to harm Mavis Spitforce, but – from her behaviour when I met her this morning – Lavinia has to be a favourite, which is why I wanted to speak with you.'

Playing for time, Bugs busied herself in pouring more tea and piling Tilly's plate with sandwiches. Suddenly, she abandoned her hostess role and sat down in one of the fireside arm chairs. 'Miss Bagshot, my dear friend Mavis had been concerned for some time about her safety. She seemed to think that she was in danger, and told me that she had uncovered a secret to do with her family. She was even thinking of moving in with that ghastly Peggledrip creature because she didn't feel safe in her own home any more.'

Tilly crammed the sandwiches into her mouth and pulled her notepad and pencil out of her cardigan pocket as Hettie began her questioning. 'When did Mavis tell you all this?'

'After the Friendship Club meeting last week. I went back to her house afterwards, and she asked me if I would witness some papers. It was awful, really, as they turned out to be copies of her will.'

'Two copies?' asked Hettie, throwing caution and cream carpet to the wind as she dunked a shortbread finger in her tea. Bugs nodded. 'Did you see what she did with the wills after you'd witnessed them?'

'No. They were still on her kitchen table when I left.'

'And did you have any idea what was in the will?'

'Not really. She didn't discuss it.'

'What about her relationship with Lavinia? Had that changed in any way recently?'

Bugs looked thoughtful, as if trying to make her mind up about something, and the pause gave Tilly time to reach for a shortbread and Hettie to revisit the last two sandwiches. 'Lavinia is . . . how shall I say this . . . a difficult cat. She's talented, intelligent and a wonderful teacher, but she has a cruel, spiteful streak about her if challenged. As I'm sure you know, Mavis brought her up because her own mother was unable to cope. She showered her with books, educated her and prepared her for the world of work. She even got her a job at the village school here in Much-Purring. The problem was a local boy cat – a different culture altogether, if you know what I mean.' Hettie hadn't the slightest idea what Bugs meant, but felt it best not to interrupt and hoped that all would become clear. 'Mavis asked me to keep an eye on Lavinia and let her lodge with me during the school terms, which didn't go down very well with Lavinia or with the boy. He suddenly started staying with his great aunt Pakora next door so that he could see Lavinia more often.'

'You mean Pakora Dosh?' Hettie clarified, pleased that the penny had finally dropped. 'So who was the boy?'

'Bhaji Dosh – Balti and Rogan's boy. Anyway, Mavis found out that Lavinia was still seeing him and washed her paws of her niece for several weeks. She moved all Lavinia's things out of her house – she brought most of them here, actually – and turned her old bedroom into a box room so that she couldn't go back.'

'How did Lavinia feel about that?'

'She was furious. Mavis had always promised her the house in Whisker Terrace, and to make matters worse, she found out that Bhaji had been promised to a very pretty Asian cat who works for Masala Dosh in Southwool.'

'Why do you think Mavis took against the friendship between Bhaji and Lavinia? The Doshes are a very rich and highly respected family, after all.'

'I don't know. Like I said, I think it was cultural differences.'

Hettie could see that there was nothing more to be

gained from that particular line of questioning, so she decided to go for the jugular. 'Miss Anderton – could you tell me what you were doing on the evening of Halloween? Just for the record, obviously.'

'I was here at home, preparing some notes for the Friendship Club.'

'And Lavinia?'

'She was away up at the school. They had a ghouls and pumpkins party, and I made some of the costumes for it. I went to my bed early, so I'm not sure what time she got back.'

Hettie shot a look at Tilly. 'What sort of costumes did you make?'

Bugs stood up and crossed the room to a wicker basket. Lifting the lid, she pulled out a cloak of orange silk. 'Several like this for the pumpkins, and white cloaks for the ghouls. Delirium Treemints helped – she made witches' hats and masks out of some black felt that she had. Pakora got the silk for us – one of the "ask no questions" special deals that we are always most grateful for.'

Tilly and Hettie stared at the orange silk and knew that they had found the maker of the cloak in which Mavis Spitforce's body had been wrapped. Hettie rose from the sofa, giving Tilly's cardigan a tug to signal that their visit was over. She took up her mac and rescued Tilly's hat, which had found its way under one of the tea trolley's wheels.

'Miss Anderton, you have been very helpful. We may need to speak with you again, so would it be possible to have your telephone number in case I think of anything else?'

'I'll give you my card,' Bugs said, reaching into a large cream handbag which was parked on the floor by her armchair. 'Please take some shortbread for your journey. I make it most days. It's a little bit of bonny Scotland that I can't seem to shake off.'

Hettie and Tilly thanked Bugs for tea and said their goodbyes, retracing their footsteps past Pakora Dosh's stores and on through the village to where they had left Bruiser and Scarlet. Bruiser had made himself comfortable out of the November chill in the sidecar and was fast asleep under a blanket, but the lure of a shortbread finger soon brought him to his senses. Refreshed and ready for the road, he helped Hettie and Tilly aboard and was preparing to mount the bike when Jacob Surplus appeared from behind an old yew tree that bordered church land.

'Oh no, not again,' groaned Hettie as the ancient ecclesiastic bore down on her, and Tilly glanced curiously at her.

'Thou shalt reap what though shalt sow,' the vicar intoned. 'The day of reckoning is but a prayer away. Repent and confess, I say to you, so that you may enter His kingdom cleansed and purified.'

Tilly threw the blanket over her head and burrowed

into her seat for warmth. Hettie stood up in the sidecar, wondering why she should have to repent over a salmon sandwich and a shortbread finger. 'Could I just stop you there?' she said as Jacob Surplus launched himself into an upbeat version of the twenty-third psalm. 'I am investigating a rather unpleasant murder which may be connected in some way to a crime that happened a very long time ago.'

Jacob stopped his singing and stared at Hettie through watery eyes. 'He's back, then. I told her not to meddle. Let sleeping cats lie lest they rise up against their tormentors.'

Although she was becoming deeply annoyed by Jacob Surplus and his religious riddles, Hettie was intrigued by what he was trying to say and attempted to gain some clarity. '*Who* has come back? And who was meddling?'

Jacob looked to his left and then to his right before answering. 'Thaddeus, come to claim another lamb for the flock buried beneath the earth. All Hallows Eve, the day of the dead.'

'And the meddler?' Hettie persisted.

'Dead,' said Jacob, looking to the heavens.

'Mavis Spitforce?'

Jacob Surplus smiled. 'Ah, the peace that comes with understanding, but first the violence. You must come and see for yourself. Tomorrow at three, perhaps?'

Hettie was bewildered and confused, but concerned

enough to accept the half-hearted invitation. Jacob melted away into the churchyard and Bruiser, looking just as bewildered as she was, kicked Scarlet into life. Hettie sat back down in the sidecar next to Tilly, who was recovering from a bout of giggling, and the three cats sped off towards the town. The daylight was fast disappearing and an already cold November day was turning icy. Bruiser took more care on the twists and turns of the road and had slowed down considerably by the time they reached the outskirts, giving Hettie and Tilly the chance to take a good long look at the Peggledrip house.

'Stop!' cried Hettie, forcing the lid of the sidecar back to let in a rush of cold air. 'There's something in that tree.'

Bruiser applied the brakes and the motorbike went into a skid, but he controlled it sufficiently to bring them to a standstill outside the gates to Peggledrip House. Hettie leapt from the sidecar and set off back down the road with Bruiser and Tilly following on behind. She had only gone a short distance before she stopped and stared in disbelief, rubbing her eyes to stem the hot tears of anger which fell uncontrollably, leaving large splashes down the front of her mac. Bruiser and Tilly caught up with her, and all three of them looked on in silence at the horror before them.

The tree was tall, part of the substantial gardens belonging to the Peggledrip house, and the few leaves and berries which still clung to it marked it out as an elder. Bruiser was the first to speak. 'Why don't you two wait in the sidecar while I sort this out? I'll 'ave to find a ladder from somewhere. There's an old orchard at the back of the house – we used to play there, stealin' apples and stuff, and there's bound to be a ladder round there.'

Hettie nodded in agreement. Bruiser took off over the boundary fence and disappeared round the back of Peggledrip House, and she tightened the belt on her mac as if that would give her strength. Sadly, she looked down at Tilly, who was still staring at the tree. 'Come on, we've got work to do. I need you to be very brave. I'll meet Bruiser at the tree if you'll go and fetch Irene Peggledrip. She needs to know about this – if she doesn't know already, by fair means or foul.'

Hettie set off back down the road, coaxing Tilly along by her cardigan. The latch on the gates to Peggledrip House gave way easily, and they opened with a resounding clank. The two cats made their way up a neglected carriage driveway, and the double-fronted house eventually revealed itself; it appeared to be in darkness, but – on closer inspection – there was a glimmer of light peeping through a curtain from one of the windows at the side of the house. Hettie pushed Tilly towards the front door. 'Just tell her something dreadful has happened in her garden. Don't tell her what – just get her out here.' Tilly set off on her mission, and Hettie strode across the lawn towards the elder tree.

By the time she reached the tree, Bruiser was approaching from the back of the house with a ladder. Looking more closely, Hettie could see that the figure hanging from the branch had been hoisted up there; the rope used had been tied around the trunk lower down to keep the body in place. The eyes were almost out of their sockets, the tongue – bitten and black – hung loosely out of the side of the mouth. The mailbag had been placed over its owner's head and hung around her neck like a grotesque bib. This was progress of sorts, thought Hettie, doing her best to hold herself together; at least Teezle Makepeace could be crossed off Tilly's list of suspects.

Bruiser secured the ladder against the tree but Hettie stopped him from going any further. 'I want Irene Peggledrip to see her before we bring her down. Tilly's fetching her now.' Looking back at the house, she could make out a lantern swinging wildly as it progressed across the lawn. Yellow wellingtons manifested themselves first, followed by the great coat and crowned by the Cossack hat; Tilly looked very small against the towering, flapping vision of Irene Peggledrip.

'Miss Bagshot! Whatever is amiss on such a night?

I was engaged in a rather hot-tempered game of backgammon with Crimola. She always has to win you see and . . .'

The medium was stopped in her tracks as she stared up at the body of Teezle Makepeace, motionless and silvered in the strengthening moon light. 'I must apologise,' she said, sinking to her knees.

For a moment Hettie thought she was going to get a confession, but Irene Peggledrip threw her arms around the tree and hugged it. 'I'm so very sorry you've been put through all this. Please give the sprites my very best wishes.'

There were moments when Hettie felt the need to stand outside herself and assess the increasingly bizarre situations in which she found herself; it was a useful trick, a bit like watching a particularly bad late night film on TV. The scene before her now bore no resemblance to anything remotely normal; Irene Peggledrip clearly inhabited a parallel universe where the indignation of trees trumped the strangled cries of an overweight post-cat. Irene struggled to her feet, satisfied that the tree bore her no lasting malice. 'I'd say about ten o'clock last night. I'll have to check with Crimola, but she didn't die here.'

Hettie marvelled at the certainty of Irene Peggledrip's words and didn't even bother to question them. She stared back up at the lifeless figure of Teezle Makepeace while Bruiser set about untying the knot from around the tree, then climbed the ladder to steady the weight as Teezle was lowered gently to the ground. Looking carefully at the body, Hettie could see that Teezle had been strangled by a piece of wire which had bitten into her neck; as Irene Peggledrip had suggested, she had obviously died before being displayed in such a horrific manner. The good news, if there was any good news, was that Teezle's death must have been quick and efficient, but why would anyone go to such lengths to kill her and then remove her body to a place which could so easily be seen from the road? It was as if the killer wanted to be noticed, to have their work appraised, and it had been the same with Mavis Spitforce: the crime scene there had been staged to look like a very bad joke.

Hettie removed the mail bag from around Teezle's neck. The undelivered letters from the day before would have to be returned to the post office with the unwelcome news that Lavender Stamp was once again looking for a new employee. Teezle's mouth was forced open by the swelling of her blackened tongue, and it was clear and refreshing to note that this time nothing had been forced into the mouth after death. Hettie wondered briefly if that was significant, but the frost was getting to everyone and she concluded her initial examinations quickly, then helped Bruiser to carry the body across the lawn under Irene Peggledrip's instruction. 'You can put her in the old dairy at the back of the house. There's a table in there, and she'll be fine overnight. Shall I give Shroud and Trestle a ring in the morning?' Straining under the weight of Teezle's body, Hettie couldn't help but think that this was turning out to be an excellent week for Shroud and Trestle. It also crossed her mind that bad luck often came in threes.

With Teezle tucked up in the old dairy, Hettie avoided any further conversation and Irene strode off to finish her game of backgammon. It was clear that she had no idea how the body had come to be strung up in her elder tree; she rarely ventured beyond her formal garden in the winter, she claimed, and had noticed nothing out of the ordinary that day. They would call on her again on Friday, as arranged, and by then one or two aspects of the case might have become clearer; there was also a strong possibility that the body count would have increased, giving Crimola even more to think about.

Bruiser drove Scarlet home, taking extra care on the icy roads, and Hettie and Tilly huddled together for warmth in the sidecar, clutching Teezle's mail bag. In spite of the darkness, Lavender Stamp was sweeping the pavement in front of the post office when they got back and Bruiser diplomatically parked the motorbike further down the High Street to avoid further caustic notes.

'Oh well, here goes,' said Hettie, grabbing the mail

bag. 'Wish me luck.' Bruiser and Tilly made their way to the Butters' shop to collect chicken pies and cream horns, all the time keeping half an eye on the goings-on outside the post office.

Lavender, who never missed the slightest movement in the High Street, was well aware of Hettie's approach; realising that she was carrying post office property, she threw her broom into the shop doorway and snatched the bag before Hettie could open her mouth. 'How dare you!' she shouted. 'It is a serious offence to interfere with the delivery of Her Majesty's mail. What do you think you are playing at? I suppose that good for nothing girl has put you up to this, too scared to face me after letting me down today. Well, you can tell Miss Teezle Makepeace from me that she won't be delivering any more post in this town. Where is she, anyway?'

Hettie couldn't resist giving the answer that came into her head. 'She'll be at Shroud and Trestle's tomorrow.'

'Shroud and Trestle's?' shrieked Lavender. 'You mean she's abandoned a career in the post office to work for a pair of disreputable undertakers?'

After such a long and difficult day, Hettie began to enjoy herself; she had suffered enough barbed insults from Lavender Stamp in the past to make this a very sweet conversation, in spite of the subject matter. 'Well, she's not exactly working for them. They're picking her up from Miss Peggledrip's old dairy in the morning.'

'What is she doing out there?' demanded Lavender, shaking with anger.

'Hanging around Miss Peggledrip's elder tree. You see, someone strangled her with a piece of wire and strung her up in the gardens of the old house. You're quite right, though – she won't be delivering any more post in this town, which is a real shame because she was very good at her job and very kind to her customers. It's a pity that more cats aren't like Teezle Makepeace. The world would be a much nicer place. So, if you do want to pay your respects, she'll be at Shroud and Trestle's tomorrow. As she was such a valued employee, you might even like to contribute to her funeral costs.' Having delivered her news, Hettie turned on her heel and crossed the road as Tilly and Bruiser emerged from the Butters', laden down with dinner. They disappeared together down the alleyway at the side of the shop, leaving Lavender Stamp staring after them – shocked, stung and bewildered, and with the smallest of tears making its way down her cheek.

CHAPTER NINE

The room was uncharacteristically cheerless when they stumbled over the threshold: the November chill had crept uninvited down the chimney, and the fire had all but gone out.

'Bloody marvellous!' said Hettie. 'After the day we've had, you'd think the fire would have stayed in to welcome us home.'

Bruiser put the food parcels down and sprang into action. 'There's still enough of a glow to get it goin' again. Leave it to me – by the time you've dished up the pies, I'll 'ave it roarin' up yer chimney.'

Tilly dragged a pile of old newspaper from

under the staff sideboard and Bruiser set about the fireplace, armed with kindling and coal. He was true to his word: by the time Hettie and Tilly had laid three places at the table for dinner and dished up the chicken pies, a healthy set of flames was licking the chimney breast and the room had begun to warm through.

Soon, there wasn't a crumb to be found on licked-clean plates, and the cats retired to the fireside to indulge themselves in Betty Butter's cream horns. Tilly switched the TV on to catch the local news. To their amazement, there seemed to be only one story. National and local TV stations were camped out on Mavis Spitforce's doorstep, covering every possible aspect of the case.

'Ooh look – there you are,' squealed Tilly in delight as Hettie stepped forward to address the crowd.

'I didn't know they were filming me,' Hettie said, admiring her first piece to camera. 'And look – there's Lavinia Spitforce. Doesn't she look cross?'

The chaos in Whisker Terrace seemed to have brought out the worst in those lucky enough to be caught on film, and many from the assembled crowd seemed keen to push themselves to the very front of the story. Balti Dosh had changed into her Dosh Stores sweatshirt and was holding court on the state of Mavis Spitforce's last days; Delirium Treemints could be seen in the background doing a roaring trade in beverages, and – as a trade-off for the constant supply of boiled kettles from the Dosh stores – had added a new line in hot samosas; and perhaps most significantly, Marmite Sprat had set her own table up, piled high with *Strange But Trues*. The camera panned across to her, focusing on the open page which detailed the story of Milky Myers.

'I don't believe it!' shouted Hettie at the television. 'They're actually going to interview her.'

Marmite Sprat stepped forward as one of the reporters forced a microphone into her face and shouted his question so that she could hear him above the crowd. 'Miss Sprat, what can you tell us about the connection between this murder and the Milky Myers case?'

Marmite cleared her throat as another dozen microphones were shoved towards her, obscuring her face almost entirely. She spoke up clearly and precisely. 'As the town's historian, I have followed up a number of interesting cases in the area, all of which are still available to buy in my *Strange But True* series of books. But there is no story so engrossing as the legend of Milky Myers, a cat who – longer ago than any of us can remember – murdered his entire family in the house on the edge of this town.' The camera cut to a picture of the Peggledrip house as Marmite Sprat continued her tale. 'The legend tells us that Milky Myers returns on Halloween to claim another victim, and that his ghost haunts several spots close by – the graveyard at Much-Purring-on-the-Rug, an old farm track, and what is now known as the Peggledrip house. It is my belief that Miss Mavis Spitforce has been murdered by Milky Myers.' With that, she held up her book and the camera moved in for a close-up. The news bulletin switched unexpectedly back to the studio, where the presenter was caught taking a bite out of a large Scotch egg. He buried it hurriedly in a pile of papers on the news desk and, with his whiskers covered in breadcrumbs, introduced the weather cat, who was still busy adding another layer of bright red lipstick to her make-up.

'What a nightmare!' said Hettie, switching the TV off. 'Are they so badly off for stories that they have to delve into the murky waters of Marmite Sprat's nonsense? Who on earth is going to believe a word of it? There's a killer out there, and all this Milky Myers stuff is blowing a convenient smokescreen across the truth. I wonder what they'll come up with when they find out about poor Teezle?'

'Legends are convenient, though, aren't they?' piped up Bruiser. 'They covers up stuff yer don't want ta admit to.'

It was rare for Bruiser to speak out, and Hettie sensed that there was something he needed to say. 'What sort of stuff?' she coaxed.

'It was bein' in that old garden today, when I fetched the ladder from the orchard. It brought it all back.' Bruiser shivered and stared into the fire as if his eyes were seeing something very far away. Tilly and Hettie sat quietly, waiting for him to continue. 'I was just a lad, really, but she looked to me for everythin'. I couldn't go out without her taggin' along, but she was no trouble – loved playin' in the sun, and I'd take her to pick the apples for Ma to make the pies. She sold them pies down the old market. We'd 'ave picnics under them old trees, when there was no one about to see.'

He struggled to find the words and only the sound of the crackling fire broke through the silence. 'It was comin' up to Halloween and we was getting under Ma's feet, so I took her for a walk to the old house. I bought her a treat on the way so's we could 'ave a winter picnic. She was playin' outside the dairy and I left her to look fer some conkers. When I gets back, she's lyin' there dead. I panicked. I didn't know what to do. She'd choked, yer see, on her Scotch egg. Ma had said she wasn't to have 'em till she was old enough to eat 'em properly, but she wanted one so bad and I bought it for her as a treat. I killed my little sister and I knew Ma would never forgive me, so I carried her home and told Ma that she'd been murdered by Milky Myers. Next thing, it was all over the town that he'd come back to haunt his old house again. I even told the newspaper man that I'd seen a face at the window of the Myers house, as was. Ma died soon after that of a broken heart. I packed up me kit and joined a circus to get as far away as possible.'

Tilly clambered off her blanket and gave Bruiser a hug, while Hettie got down from her chair and put the kettle on. 'No one can blame you for what you did,' she said. 'The Milky Myers story was a perfect way of explaining a tragic accident, and the fact that it's gone into the town's history is more to do with the stupidity of those who were old enough to know better. You've only got to look at the rubbish we've just seen on the news to see how a few careless words can create a distorted picture of the facts.' Bruiser took comfort from Hettie's words and Tilly's hugs, and somehow felt better for his confession. It had all happened many years ago, but the death of his little sister had cast a long shadow across his life, and it had been easier to run from the truth than to face up to the reality of what Hettie rightly called a tragic accident.

Hettie returned to the fire with three steaming mugs of tea, determined to thrash out the possibilities of the case before it got any worse. She had just reached for her catnip pouch and begun to fill her pipe when Tilly sprang from her blanket, nearly spilling hot tea all over Bruiser, who had settled down with his chin on the fender. 'I've just remembered,' she cried excitedly. 'We've got a parcel. It's here somewhere.' At some stage in the day the parcel had fallen under the table, but after a certain amount of scuffling and sneezing Tilly emerged with her prize.

'I'm not sure we've time for a parcel,' said Hettie, blowing three perfect smoke rings and passing the pipe to Bruiser.

Tilly refused to be put off and dragged the parcel over to her blanket where she clawed at the string and brown paper until it gave way to reveal a collection of papers and sealed envelopes. The first envelope was addressed to Hettie. 'It's full of stuff, but this one's for you,' Tilly said.

Hettie looked over at the bundle of papers and yawned. 'I'm too tired to deal with stuff tonight, and I need to have a good think about this bloody case. If you want to open the letter, be my guest, but if it's more trouble I don't want to know.'

Tilly wasted no time in opening the envelope and shook the contents onto her blanket. 'It's money, and lots of it! Look!'

Hettie stared in disbelief and suddenly became interested. 'There must be thirty or forty pounds there. Is there a note to say who it's from?'

Tilly sorted through the money, counting as she went, and pulled a blue piece of paper out of the middle of the banknotes. 'There's fifty pounds actually, and the letter is from Miss Spitforce!'

'Which one?'

'The dead one. Shall I read it to you?'

Before Hettie could answer, Bruiser stood up. 'I think I'm ready for me bed. Got me old bones warmed through nicely so I'll get off to me shed. Will we be out and about tomorrow?'

'Yes, we will,' said Hettie, getting up to show him to the door. 'And thank you for today. I hope you sleep well, and don't let the frost get to you.' Bruiser bid them both goodnight and made his way down the garden, more content than he'd been for many years. Now his secret was out, he felt that he could properly grieve for his sister and his mother, and having good friends around him made all the difference.

'Right,' said Hettie, closing the door and padding back to her chair. 'Let's have it then. What has Mavis Spitforce got to say from beyond the grave?'

Tilly cleared her throat and squinted down at the letter:

Sunday 30th October

My dear Miss Bagshot,
Enclosed is a retainer for your services on a matter that has been troubling me for some time. I would be most grateful if you could find the time to call on me this Friday so that I may discuss my concerns in detail with you.

I have included in the parcel a number of

papers that are no longer safe in my home. I would be obliged if you would look through them. I also enclose a copy of my will in the hope that – should anything happen to me – you will see that my wishes are carried out to the letter.

These are difficult times. There are those who would prefer me to remain silent, but with your help I hope that justice will finally be done and the innocent be vindicated.

Yours sincerely,
Mavis Spitforce

Hettie sat for a moment deep in thought while Tilly gathered up the banknotes and put them in a neat pile on the staff sideboard. She scrunched up the brown paper and put it by the coal scuttle, ready for burning, then returned to her blanket to look through the papers that Miss Spitforce had sent. First, she pulled out a long envelope which she suspected was the will mentioned in the letter; opening it, she was satisfied that it was a copy of the one that Lavinia Spitforce had destroyed earlier.

Hettie refilled her pipe, trying to avoid the wave of tiredness that was engulfing her. They had had a very early start, and the day was still presenting surprises.

'Anything else of interest in that stuff?'

'I'm not really sure. The will's here, so that's a smack in the face for Lavinia.'

'Couldn't happen to a nicer soul,' muttered Hettie. 'What are all those old bits of paper you've got there?'

'They're from various churches,' Tilly said, trying to read a selection of impossible handwriting. 'Burial records, I think. Miss Spitforce loved doing this sort of thing, didn't she? Oh and there's a map.' Tilly nearly disappeared from view altogether as she unfolded the map across the hearth.

Hettie stared down at it. 'She must have done this herself – look at all the crosses and marks she's put on it, some in blue and some in red. I can't make out what it is, though. There are little boxes next to the blue crosses, and there's a definite road running through it all, but the whole thing seems to be in some sort of Spitforce code. What's in that notebook you're sitting on?'

Tilly passed the notebook to Hettie and set about attempting to refold the map. It was several minutes before she managed to bring the creature to heel, singeing one of the corners in the process. For fear it may rear up again, she slid it under the coal scuttle.

'Well, this is interesting,' said Hettie, looking up from the notebook. 'It looks like her own investigation into the Milky Myers case. There are statements from cats who were around at the time, and she's even sketched out the milk round and started it from the Myers' house all the way to Much-Purring. Look – the farm track's been marked with a red cross, so maybe the red crosses on that map are murder sites. There are five around the Myers' house – that must be the rest of the family.'

Getting excited, Tilly leapt from her blanket and sat on the arm of Hettie's chair so that she could look over her shoulder. 'Who are all those other cats she's listed on that page?' she asked. 'They've all got initials after them: Tubbs MPS; Bundle MPB; Winkle MPC; Slipper MPC; and Pump MPM. Wait a minute – I'm sure there was a Slipper mentioned in one of those church letters.'

Returning to the avalanche of papers on her blanket, she retrieved the church correspondence. 'Yes, here it is – Lily Slipper, died three years ago, buried in St Savouries Churchyard in Much-Purring-on-the-Cushion. Here's another one – Osbert Tubbs, five years ago, buried in St Whiskers' churchyard in Much-Purring-on-the-Step. That's it! The MPs are villages, and all these cats have died in the last few years according to the burial records.'

'Well done,' said Hettie in a rare moment of admiration. 'I think we should put the milk on for the cocoa. There's so much to think about and we need a good night's sleep. We must take another look at that map in the morning when we're awake enough to understand it, and I think a spin round the villages tomorrow afternoon might help. We mustn't forget that there's a killer out there and Miss Spitforce has inadvertently paid us well over the odds to find out who it is. And then there's the vicar of Much-Purring-on-the-Rug – I'll need to talk to him, heaven help me, and have a good look around his churchyard. It's going to be another long day.'

CHAPTER TEN

Hettie woke from a heavy sleep to the smell of bacon. Opening one eye, she focused on the clock on the staff sideboard which confirmed her suspicions – she had overslept. It was gone nine and the No. 2 Feline Detective Agency had detected very little so far other than a pair of bacon baps which her other eye located just out of reach on the table.

'Oh bugger!' said Tilly, as an unruly tea bag splashed back into the mug she was retrieving it from. 'It's a shame tea leaves are such a mess. They're much kinder, and you don't get scalded when things go wrong.' Hettie wasn't sure whether to join in the conversation or not, but decided against it as Tilly seemed to be handling the debate perfectly well on her own. 'Of course, there's the tea pot issue,' she continued, warming to her theme. 'Extra washing up, and the second cup out of the pot always tastes nasty. Then there's the cosy or no cosy situation – I suppose if I were a teapot I'd want a cardigan to keep me warm.'

The smell of bacon had become unbearable and Tilly's soliloquy over the teapot was a little too surreal for Hettie to cope with at this time of day. 'I think we should stick with the tea bags and break out the bacon baps,' she said.

Tilly looked up from her tea-making. 'Oh good, you're awake. Bruiser brought these in for us as a thank you for last night. He's taken his down the shed because he didn't want to wake you, but he said to give him a shout when we're ready to go out in Scarlet.'

Hettie yawned and stretched. Pulling her dressing gown on, she made her way towards the baps as Tilly added two mugs of hot tea to the breakfast table. Their room was much tidier than Hettie remembered it. She'd fallen into a deep sleep surrounded by Miss Spitforce's papers, dirty dinner plates and hurriedly discarded clothes; now, all was in its place and the Spitforce papers were stacked neatly at the other end of the table, waiting for them to start work. Tilly had clearly been busy in Hettie's slumbering absence, and the two cats sat and enjoyed their extra-large bacon baps before another word was said.

They spent the morning poring over Miss Spitforce's map. It was clear that the red crosses were sites where cats had died; the blue crosses seemed to correspond with the Much-Purring villages; and the boxes were still a puzzle. Tilly jotted down details of the burial records, matching up deceased cats with their villages so that they could refer to them later when they went out.

'That's a good morning's work,' said Hettie, stretching. 'I think we should pay a call on Balti Dosh and Marmite Sprat before we set off for the Much-Purrings. I'll go and get Bruiser while you pop to the Butters' and get us something nice for lunch. You'd better order supper, too – I'm not sure what time we'll be back.'

Tilly skipped round to the front of the shop to find the lunchtime queue in full swing, which gave her plenty of time to decide what she would buy when her turn came. Betty and Beryl ran their business like a well-oiled machine, making sure that the shop was stacked to the gills with freshly baked pies, breads and cakes ready for the town's hungry hordes. They also supplied the food hall at Malkin and Sprinkle with their 'Tastes Lovely' range, which sold out most days before eleven o'clock. Mr Sprinkle had wanted to treble the order but Betty and Beryl – being shrewd business cats as well as master bakers – knew that once the pies had sold out in the food hall, customers would make the trek down to the other end of the High Street to their shop, where the profit margin was higher and their full range of sweets and savouries would tempt additional sales. Such was the popularity of their wares that they invariably wiped their surfaces down by half past three, giving them plenty of time to put their feet up or pop out to the local garden centre for a nice cup of tea and a look round; both sisters were keen gardeners, growing vegetables and flowers in perfect harmony in the sizeable plot at the back of their bakery.

As the queue moved forward, Tilly watched the cream horns and custard tarts diminish before her very eyes. There were plenty of Eccles cakes and ring doughnuts left, but she had no time for cakes with holes where the cream should be and couldn't see the point in currants at all.

'Now then, Miss Tilly,' said Beryl. 'What will it be today? Sausage pie's the special.'

'Ooh yes, that would be lovely. I'll need three, as Bruiser is still with us.'

'So I see,' said Beryl, placing three pies in a bag. 'He gave us a hand with the coal this morning, then helped Betty dig the last of the spuds. Useful sort to have around. And pudding?'

'I don't suppose there are three cream horns left,

are there?' asked Tilly, seeing that the tray was now empty.

'You might be in luck.' Betty joined her sister at the counter. 'I put these by when you walked in.'

Tilly clapped her paws with delight. 'Oh and I'll need three rolls for lunch – cheese would be nice.'

Betty took up her butter knife, selected three large rolls, and filled them with sizeable wedges of cheese as Beryl added up the bill. Tilly handed over her luncheon vouchers and paid the extra, staggering under the sheer weight of the cakes, pies and rolls. She turned to leave, and walked straight into Marmite Sprat who was behind her in the queue.

'Oh Miss Sprat – I wonder if you might have time to pop into our office at the back of the bakery for a few minutes? Miss Bagshot is keen to talk to you.'

Marmite eyed Tilly with suspicion as Beryl waited patiently for her order. 'I'll have an Eccles cake and a plain bridge roll, please,' she said, not even looking at Beryl. 'I'm rather busy today with matters pertaining to my book,' she added, obviously hoping to dismiss Tilly as quickly as possible.

'But Miss Sprat, it's your lovely book that we want to talk about.'

'Very well, then, but five minutes is all I can spare.' Marmite snatched her frugal lunch from the counter, giving Beryl the exact money, and followed Tilly out of the bakery and round to the Butters' backyard.

Hettie was on her way up the path with Bruiser, kitted out in his leathers; seeing that Tilly had bagged a prime suspect, she sent him off to prepare Scarlet for her outing.

'Miss Sprat – how lovely to see you,' she said with as much charm as she could muster. 'Please come through to the office.'

The smell of bacon hung in the air, but that was the only hint of domestic bliss – or chaos – and Hettie was relieved to see that their room really did look like an office, with papers stacked neatly on the table.

'Please take a seat, Miss Sprat. Forgive us for the limited space – we're looking for bigger premises but are too snowed under with work to do much about it.'

Tilly suppressed a giggle, marvelling at Hettie's talent for knowing how to impress. Her words were lost on Marmite Sprat, who grudgingly perched herself on the edge of the proffered chair.

'Miss Sprat,' Hettie began, knowing that a spot of ego massaging was the only way to go with their unwilling visitor, 'first let me congratulate you on your latest book. I have thoroughly enjoyed reading it and would love you to sign my copy before you go.'

Tilly pulled the book out from under the staff sideboard and brushed the crumbs off, thankful that Marmite was facing the other way. She put it on the desk and took up her notepad and pencil ready for Hettie's questioning. Marmite eyed her book nervously, and Hettie – seeing that niceties weren't washing – got stuck in. 'I'm interested in your theory regarding the death of Miss Mavis Spitforce. I was surprised to see an intelligent cat like you on the news last night telling everyone that Milky Myers was responsible.'

Marmite was shocked at the change in Hettie's tone; it had become confrontational, and not at all to her liking. 'Miss Bagshot, it may suit you and your friends to go about this town poking your noses into things that don't concern you under the pretence of being detectives, but some of us see through that nonsense. Your so-called talk at the Friendship Club was amateurish to say the least, and now you seem to think you are investigating Mavis Spitforce's death. I would like to know who has appointed you to that position.'

Hettie stared at the thin, pinched brown cat before her, wondering how best to deliver the slap she surely had coming to her. 'Our agency has been retained to investigate a number of circumstances surrounding Miss Spitforce's death by Miss Spitforce herself.'

'You must think I'm stupid,' scoffed Marmite. 'Messages from beyond the grave? That's pure Peggledrip rubbish.'

Hettie was beginning to enjoy herself. 'Ah, Miss Peggledrip has been most helpful with our enquiries but Miss Spitforce was very much alive when she engaged us. And yes, I do think you're stupid to believe that Milky Myers – or Thaddeus, to give him his proper name – has come back from the dead to murder his great, great granddaughter.'

'Stuff and nonsense,' said Marmite, getting up to leave. 'You're making it up to discredit me and my book.'

'I assure you we have proof positive that Mavis Spitforce was related to Thaddeus Myers, and as for making it up, I rather think that's your department. Might I suggest you start a new series of books called *Strange But False*? That should go down well with your friends at the Methodist Hall. And before you go, I'd like to know where you were on the night of Halloween, just to eliminate you from our enquiries.'

Tilly moved in with her notepad, pencil poised and ready to write.

'How dare you suggest I had anything to do with Mavis Spitforce's death! I didn't like her, that's perfectly true – she always thought she was so much better than everyone else, her and Bugs Anderton bossing us all round at the club, making fools of us in front of the guest speakers.'

Hettie knew that the venom pouring from Marmite Sprat was going to be endless unless she stemmed the flow. 'So where were you on Halloween?' she repeated with a little more force.

'I was at home all night, like I am every night. I lock and bolt my door at six o'clock, and retire with a book by half past eight.'

Hettie couldn't help but think that Marmite Sprat had no real need to lock and bolt her door; why would anyone want to intrude on such an inhospitable shrew? But she resisted and moved on to other questions that needed answering. 'And were you at home on Tuesday evening after the Friendship Club?'

'As I have said, I'm always at home in the evenings. Now, if you've quite finished, I have books to pack up and get in the post.'

Hettie ignored Marmite's wish to leave and continued with her questions. 'Did you discuss your new book with Mavis Spitforce?'

'No I didn't. I sent her a copy in the post.'

'Why?'

'Because she'd told Delirium Treemints that she was also writing a book on the Myers case. I wanted her to see that I'd got there first. She was always belittling the things I did.'

'So has it come as a shock to you that Mavis Spitforce was related to Thaddeus Myers?'

'Even if she was, that still doesn't mean my story is wrong. He murdered his entire family, and if Mavis *was* family, that rather proves my theory, doesn't it?' Marmite Sprat stood up, satisfied with her parting shot. She grabbed her meagre lunch rations from Hettie's desk and made for the door.

Hettie waited until their visitor's footsteps had faded away across the backyard before speaking her mind. 'Bloody opportunist! She'd say anything to sell a book – historian my foot! But I doubt she's a murderer. She's not clever enough.'

'Shall we cross her off the list?' asked Tilly, packing the cheese rolls into her shoulder bag.

'Not just yet, but I honestly can't see her garrotting Teezle Makepeace and swinging her from an elder tree. That's far too imaginative for Marmite Sprat.'

Bruiser was busy polishing Scarlet with an old handkerchief when Hettie and Tilly joined him. He'd plumped up the cushions in the sidecar and was busy buffing up the chrome around the headlight.

'She looks lovely,' said Tilly, clambering into her seat and making sure not to squash the rolls in her bag.

'Dosh Stores in Whisker Terrace first,' Hettie instructed, jumping in beside her and closing the lid.

Bruiser moved out into the lunchtime traffic and sped down the High Street, noticing that the petrol gauge was close on empty. Calculating that he could get to Whisker Terrace first, he dropped Hettie and Tilly outside the stores and drove off to fill up at the pump in Lazarus Hambone's yard.

The street was much quieter than the day before. There was no sign of anyone outside the Spitforce house, which gave Hettie the opportunity she'd hoped for. 'I need to collect those true crime books from Mavis's before we talk to Balti Dosh,' she said. 'Stand guard for me. I won't be long.'

Tilly tucked herself in behind Mavis Spitforce's hedge as Hettie made her way round to the back of the house. She took the key from her mac pocket and let herself into the kitchen. The house was silent and desolate. As Hettie passed through the rooms, she witnessed much evidence of Lavinia's ransacking: drawers were open, small homely treasures tossed into boxes, and upstairs a mountain of clothes was piled high on Mavis's bed as if nothing mattered except the bricks and mortar. Hettie was almost disappointed not to find Lavinia there, deconstructing her aunt's life; she would have relished the opportunity to wave the copy of the new will at her, but that could wait.

She pushed the door of the box room open and quickly found what she was looking for – a lavish, beautifully bound set of true crime books, Mavis Spitforce's gift to Balti Dosh. There were eight volumes in total, covering over a hundred years of crime and detailing the investigations and outcomes from a detective's perspective. Hettie hugged them to her, wishing that Mavis had seen fit to leave them to the No. 2 Feline Detective Agency, but the will had to be served, and served it would be.

Locking the house and retaining the key, Hettie staggered into Whisker Terrace under the weight of Balti's bequest. Tilly came to the rescue as the top two books in her arms made a bid for freedom. 'Good catch!' she said, leading the way to the Dosh

Stores. There was never a time when the shop wasn't busy: Rogan and Balti took it in turns to keep it open eighteen hours a day, closing only on their holy days, and then only briefly to partake in any necessary ceremonial occasions. They were the lifeblood of the Terrace and surrounding area, and very much part of the community. Like all their relatives, they worked hard with an unshaken pride and determination to stock and supply everything that their customers required.

Rogan was at the helm of his empire when Hettie and Tilly entered the shop, and it was some time before he was able to attend to them. Tilly marvelled at his skill with the bacon slicer, and his deftness with the cheese wire on a large block of cheddar was mesmerising. One by one, his customers left with baskets full to bursting, and at last Hettie's turn came.

'Good morning Miss Bagshot, how very lovely to see you,' Rogan said, giving the broadest of welcoming smiles. 'What is your desire from my shop today?'

Hettie felt that after such a welcome she should look for something to buy, but suddenly remembered why she was there. 'I'm afraid we're not shopping today, Mr Dosh, but I do have a delivery for Balti if she's around?'

Rogan eyed up the stack of books. 'Goodness! I am not sure we have ordered such books. I think there has been a jolly mistake.'

Hettie's arms were beginning to ache as Balti herself bustled through from a room at the back of the shop, carrying a tray of freshly baked samosas. Rogan melted away at her appearance and returned to his bacon slicer.

'Miss Bagshot! What a truly nice surprise. Are you detecting today?' Balti asked eagerly as she slammed the batch of samosas down onto the counter.

'Yes, we are, and I would be most grateful for a few moments of your time – in private, if possible.'

Balti looked a little startled but recovered her composure. 'Yes, of course. Please come through to the back room. You can leave your books behind the counter.'

'Actually, they're your books – that's one of the reasons we've come to see you.'

Balti's eyes lit up. 'For me? These beautiful books? How can that be possible?'

Hettie waited to reply until she and Tilly had been installed on an old sofa in Balti's back room come kitchen, which was obviously the hub of all things Dosh. There was a giant kitchen range with two industrial sized pans bubbling away on top, filling the room with the most tantalising aroma of blended spices. The large kitchen table was covered in flour from a recent rolling out session, and the remaining space was filled with boxes and crates of stock waiting to be put out on the shelves as and when required.

Hettie cut straight to the point of her visit while Tilly stacked the books neatly in the only vacant corner the room offered. 'I have been asked to be the executor of Miss Spitforce's will, and she has left you this very fine collection of books.'

Hettie had hardly finished her sentence before Balti pounced on her windfall, sniffing them first and then turning the pages with such relish that Tilly thought she was actually going to take a bite out of one. 'Oh my,' she purred. 'Just look at all these pictures – close-ups of bodies, murder weapons and crime scenes. What jolly fun I will have!'

Balti seemed to be in a world of her own, and Hettie knew that the spell must be broken before the Indian cat was lost totally to the lurid and graphic pages of her new crime library. 'While we are here, I wonder if we might ask a few questions concerning Miss Spitforce's death?' she asked, signalling to Tilly to open her notebook.

'Of course.' Balti abandoned her books and perched on a kitchen chair. 'I must tell you that I know nothing. I have been most busy with the shop, and even though she lives next door, I saw nothing.'

She seemed to think that this mantra of denial concluded her interview, but Hettie refused to be so easily diverted from her path. 'I'm more interested in your friendship with Mavis Spitforce. I understand that there had been a problem with your son, Bhaji, and Mavis's niece, Lavinia. Did that affect your relationship with Miss Spitforce?'

Balti suddenly looked angry. 'That is all water under the bridge. Bhaji is to marry a distant cousin. It has all been arranged and he will do what his grandfather tells him or he won't get his own shop.'

Hettie decided to continue with her theme. 'I understand that Pakora Dosh encouraged Bhaji and Lavinia to see each other. How did you feel about that?'

'Aunt Pakora is a law unto herself. She has her own agenda, and it's all family – you wouldn't understand. Anyway, what has Bhaji to do with this?'

'Bugs Anderton told me that Mavis Spitforce sent Lavinia away so that she couldn't see Bhaji any more. Mavis was obviously unhappy about the relationship.'

'Mavis and I were friends. She never spoke to me about Bhaji and Lavinia. Bugs Anderton has no business to speak of my family. All I can say is that one day Lavinia moved out to stay with Miss Anderton in Much-Purring-on-the-Rug and she never came back. If you want to know any more, you'll have to ask Pakora, but don't tell her I sent you. Bhaji is her favourite, and she sees no wrong in him. Like I said – it's all family.'

'And do you see any wrong in him?'

'He is my son and I love him, but I am not his future. Others in the family will decide what he is to be and where his life will lead. I am only a very small part of this family. My life was arranged for me when I was a small kitten, and it is a path I must follow.'

Hettie sensed that Balti was about to open her heart, and the pretty Asian cat looked suddenly fragile and vulnerable; the forthright bravado had disappeared, and she stared down at her sandaled feet as if deciding what to say next. The moment was stolen by a noisy interjection from Rogan. 'Balti! I must insist that you take your place at the counter. Aunt Pakora is here to collect the samosas and she wishes to speak with me on urgent business. Please ask your guests to leave.'

Balti stood and recovered herself immediately. 'Please excuse me,' she said, ushering Hettie and Tilly back into the shop. 'I am most grateful for the books.' She took up her position behind the counter, and Hettie and Tilly made their way back into Whisker Terrace where Rogan and Pakora seemed to be having a heated conversation outside the shop. Pakora's tricycle appeared to have suffered a puncture due to some broken glass left carelessly on the pavement, and the two cats had launched themselves into an excited exchange in their native tongue.

'You wouldn't want to be on the end of that, would you?' muttered Hettie, leading Tilly away from the altercation by her cardigan. 'Poor Balti. Not much of a life for her.'

'Especially as she sweeps up outside the shop. She

obviously missed that piece of glass, so let's hope she's good at mending punctures.'

Bruiser swung round the corner on Scarlet, having fuelled her up in Hambone's yard. He parked outside Miss Spitforce's house, giving the argument outside the Dosh stores a very wide berth; Pakora was now bombarding Rogan with vegetables and screaming like a banshee.

'Let's get out of here!' shouted Hettie as she and Tilly clambered into the sidecar. 'Much-Purring-on-the-Rug and lunch, I think.'

Bruiser closed the lid on the sidecar, spun round on Scarlet and headed out of town in time to see Shroud and Trestle's removals van pull out of Irene Peggledrip's driveway. 'There goes Teezle,' shouted Tilly above the raw of the engine. 'I'm pleased she ate our pie before she went. It was her last supper, really.'

Hettie didn't answer. Something was bothering her, and she remained deep in thought until Bruiser pulled over in Much-Purring-on-the-Rug. There was an old bench in the lay-by, and Tilly decided that it would be a good place for them to eat their cheese rolls, despite the cold. To add to the feast, Bruiser had purchased a flagon of Meridian Hambone's homemade ginger beer, which lurked in a large tank with a tap next to the petrol pump in their yard. Some would say that Meridian's fiery ginger beer was capable of powering any type of combustion engine and could, at a pinch, do away with the need for petrol altogether; for Hettie, Tilly and Bruiser, it served as a warming treat on a day that looked increasingly like snow.

'What's to be done next?' asked Bruiser through a mouthful of cheese.

'Well, I'm going to take a look round the village and have a word with the old vicar,' said Hettie, flicking crumbs off her business slacks. 'I think we're going to have to split up to get everything done today. If you take Tilly on a tour of the other villages to check out these deaths that Mavis Spitforce was looking into, you can pick me up here later.'

Tilly was over-excited at the prospect of a real outing in Scarlet. Having drunk more than her fair share of Meridian Hambone's ginger beer, she lapsed into a violent bout of hiccups, bursting one of the buttons off her cardigan which Bruiser rescued from the road seconds before an old farm cat drove past on his tractor. With the lunch break over, she clambered back into the sidecar and prepared for her journey around the Much-Purring clutch of villages. Armed with Mavis Spitforce's unruly map and the ever-present notepad and pencil, Tilly and Bruiser roared off on their adventure, leaving Hettie to kick her heels until her three o'clock assignation in the churchyard.

She shivered as a gust of icy wind whipped up around her. It was one of those raw November days with no promise of sunshine, just a deepening, progressive gloom. The golden days of October had given way to the deathly stillness of a world without hope – a world bracing itself for the cruel reality of winter. The church clock struck two with a shivering clunk. Hettie pulled her collar up, tightened her belt and dug her paws deeply into her mac pockets, then set off for a brisk walk into the village. She hadn't got very far before she found the note she had stuffed into her pocket after removing it from Mavis's box of sovereigns. She pulled it out and slipped into a bus shelter to read it. The note was short and to the point:

Dear Mildred,
These coins are all that is left of our past. They are very valuable – sell them and make a good life for yourself. Keep an eye on Lavinia. I fear she may be in danger.
    Mavis

Hettie folded the note and put it back in her pocket. So the coins were a legacy from the past, but why should Lavinia Spitforce be in danger? It occurred to her that out of all the cats involved in this case, Lavinia was one of the few who were perfectly capable of looking after themselves. Pondering on many aspects of the crimes, she walked on into the centre of the village and couldn't resist crossing the road to take a closer look at the Dosh Stores. Through the over-cluttered shop window, she could see that Bhaji Dosh was holding the fort while his great aunt Pakora sorted out her transport problems in the town; it was an opportunity not to be missed. Picking up a copy of the *Daily Snout* from the newspaper stand, and ignoring the photograph of Marmite Sprat brandishing her book on the front page, Hettie made her way into the shop to be greeted by a wall of sitar music. Bhaji was obviously amusing himself whilst the cat was away.

For Hettie, memories of a different life came flooding back. 'I love this music,' she said, going up to the counter. 'I once played a festival with Ravi Shancat and his whole Indian orchestra.'

Bhaji looked up from the magazine he was reading and beamed at Hettie. 'That's truly amazing. He's my favourite player. What was he like?'

Hettie thought for a moment, looking for the right word to describe the world's most famous exponent of the sitar. And then it came to her. 'Serene – serene and spiritual. It was hard to separate him from his music, if you know what I mean.'

Surprisingly, Bhaji knew exactly what Hettie meant and she could see that they had discovered some common ground to build on. 'I have my own sitar in the back – would you like to see it?' he asked, taking the money for the newspaper.

'That would be great. I haven't been close to one for years.' Hettie began to forget why she was there as Bhaji sprang from his counter and returned seconds later, wielding the long-necked instrument. He sat cross-legged on the floor and gave Hettie a short but rather beautiful accompaniment to the already deafening sound of piped music, but the impromptu concert was brought to an abrupt end by the arrival of Bugs Anderton in search of some frozen peas.

Bhaji leapt to his feet, dragging the sitar to a space behind the counter, and Bugs made a beeline for Hettie. 'Miss Bagshot – what a very pleasant surprise! I see you've been treated to one of young Bhaji's talents, although I doubt that Pakora would approve of such goings-on in her main concourse.' Bugs smiled across at Bhaji and winked. 'Not that anyone here is likely to tell her. What the eye doesn't see . . .'

Bhaji looked as though he was used to sharing secrets with Bugs, and when the time came for her to pay for her peas, a rare Dosh discount was applied to her bill. Bugs paid up and took Hettie's arm, leading her to the door. 'Miss Bagshot,' she said conspiratorially, lowering her voice to a barely audible murmur, 'how does your case proceed? Are you any closer to finding the culprit?'

Hettie decided to use the official line. 'Since we last spoke, a number of new leads have emerged which we are now following up. I'm confident of a breakthrough very soon.' This was said more for her own benefit than for Bugs's; in truth, the plot was thickening by the minute. Bugs left with her peas and Hettie returned to her conversation with Bhaji. 'You seem very keen on your music. Aren't you tempted to take it up professionally? It's a great life on the road – concerts, festivals, living the high life.'

Bhaji shook his head. 'I was born into the wrong family for that. We are shopkeepers.'

Hettie remembered what Balti had said earlier. 'But surely you can take some time out for a few adventures before running the family store? You have a talent for music and you should use it. The world would be a very sad place if we just had shopkeepers.'

'That's what my ex-girlfriend said. She became a teacher because her aunt said she had to. We hoped to have some adventures together but it wasn't to be.'

Hettie began to understand some of the anger she'd witnessed in her meeting with Lavinia Spitforce – enough anger to kill, perhaps. 'That's a real shame. Do you still see her?'

Bhaji hung his head. 'No, she hates me. My family has arranged for me to marry one of my cousins and she thinks I've given her up for another cat, which isn't true. I will love Lavinia till my dying day.'

There was a screech of breaks outside the shop as Pakora Dosh brought her tricycle to a halt just short of the vegetable racks. Bhaji looked fearful and turned the music down to an irritating background level. Realising that to be seen twice in a Dosh store looked a little obvious, Hettie said a hurried goodbye and moved out of sight behind the greetings card fixture just as Pakora Dosh blew through the door in a swirl of bright red sari, looking even more bad tempered than when Hettie had last seen her. 'Get that music off you stupid boy! We're not running a jukebox here. Have you been wasting your time playing that instrument? How much money have you taken today?'

Hettie chose her moment to creep out of the shop, leaving Bhaji to his fate, and retraced her footsteps through the village. It was almost time for her meeting with the Reverend Jacob Surplus. She had no patience with religion of any sort: to believe in something that seemed to cause so much trouble in the world seemed utterly pointless, and the trappings of belief that stood out in every town and village across the land – churches, huge rectories, even Methodist halls – all spoke of a piety that didn't seem to be able to touch those who truly needed help and comfort. In her opinion, there were many questions to be answered by the legion of holy representatives who fooled their diminishing flocks into thinking that the next life would be better as long as they behaved themselves in this one; then there were those who railroaded through life, making everyone else's existence hell on earth and then – by conveniently apologising in a confessional – receiving joyful absolution and free passage into the glories of the kingdom of heaven.

On a more practical basis, Hettie found it very hard to embrace an institution that locked its doors against the biting winters, yet was happy to provide funerals for cats who froze to death on the streets. It seemed a matter of common sense to her that these vast buildings of worship should throw their doors open on cold nights and fire up their kitchens with hot soup and a constant supply of warm blankets; a simple thought, but obviously alien to the select band of do-gooders who trooped in on Sundays, fought over the flower arranging rotas, cleansed themselves with a verse or two from a mysterious black book, belted out a few rousing tunes, then returned home to their perfect little houses free of all obligation to their fellow cats.

Architecturally, the church of Our Lady and St Biscuit was the crowning glory of the village. It rose out of the churchyard like a giant ship, its spire pointing to the heavens and its stained glass windows watchful over earthly matters. Hettie loved graveyards with a passion. It was the names on the stones that excited her, and in the days when she had written songs for her band, she had spent many a happy hour trawling through the long-forgotten epitaphs in search of inspiration, lifting a name here and there, and giving a whole new existence to the long-dead through her songs; 'Silas the Silent', 'Victoria by the Window' and her big hit, 'White Witch', all had names or lines borrowed from monuments to the fallen.

The churchyard of St Biscuit's was a delight. Avoiding the path which led to the church, Hettie struck out across the grass, enthralled by the collection of gravestones and memorials engulfed by nature, overgrown with vines and twisted roots, and reshaped by a constant battering from the weather. There was no sign of Jacob Surplus, but she was early and pleased to have some peaceful time to reflect on the ever-expanding problem of Mavis Spitforce's murder; standing in a place where death held no mystery made her consider how easy it would be to end a life and walk away, justifying your actions with no fear of retribution. The cat who had killed Mavis and Teezle was at this moment going about his or her daily tasks, perhaps even helping Hettie with her enquiries and laughing behind her back. The puzzle was coming together, but one or two pieces were hidden from view; without them, the full picture refused to emerge.

St Biscuit's clunked an apology for three o'clock and Hettie was suddenly aware that she was no longer alone. She scanned the graveyard for signs of life, but could see no one. Retracing her footsteps to the place where she had first met the cleric, she missed the path and found herself in a much older section of the churchyard. The stones were crumbling and hard to read but – where a date was still legible – they testified to housing the dead of longer ago than anyone could remember. Hettie faltered as she felt the hackles rise on the back of her neck; someone was watching her. Trying to look unconcerned, she focused on some of the old gravestones, watchful all the time for anything around her that moved. The silence was deafening and the first expected flakes of snow began to swirl around her, getting thicker all the time, settling on her whiskers and blinding her eyes. She had lost all direction and searched desperately for the church, the only tangible landmark which could lead her back to the path; it was nowhere in sight and she began to panic, wishing she'd brought Bruiser and Tilly as backup. Then, as if by divine intervention, the snow stopped. Hettie rubbed her eyes, relieved to have a clear vision of her surroundings once more, and looked to her right. Several yards away, Jacob Surplus stood amid a clutch of old gravestones. He waved his stick in her direction, and Hettie moved forward to greet him.

'How goes you on this day?' asked Jacob. 'I trust we are well met at this hour.'

Hettie was intrigued by his quaint turn of phrase and grateful for the lack of sermon in his greeting. 'I'm very well, thank you. And pleased that the snow has stopped.'

Jacob stared at the sky, then back at Hettie. 'You will know more if you come closer to me. There are things you must see.' Hettie made her way towards him, noticing that he was standing in the centre of a ring of gravestones which all bore the same name and date: this was the final resting place of the murdered Myers family. Jacob smiled, satisfied with Hettie's recognition of the burial plot. 'So, my dear – you are the chosen one,' he said, taking her arm for the grand tour. Raising his stick, he pointed to each grave in turn as they moved round the inside of the ring of stones, chanting the names of the departed. 'Matthew, Eliza, Isaac, Thomasina, Peregrine and Arabella – sacrificed so that others may prosper.'

Hettie stared at the graves and then at Jacob Surplus. 'Do you believe that Thaddeus Myers killed his family?'

'Ask him,' replied Jacob. 'He is so often here. He cries for their souls and waits for an avenging angel to come.'

Hettie desperately wanted a straight answer but resigned herself to playing along. 'And was Mavis Spitforce that avenging angel, do you think?'

'She searches for the truth, but now the truth is found, more lies will follow. She is at peace, but leaves a troubled path.'

Hettie tried a new tactic. 'Do you know who killed Mavis Spitforce?'

Jacob put his head on one side as if thinking up an answer. 'It is not for me to say. These things are beyond my time. I am the messenger. I bring you no wisdom, just the knowledge that Thaddeus weeps for the souls of his kin. He hides in the church until it is safe to leave. He knows they will hunt him down and kill him.' Jacob pointed his stick across at the church. 'Sanctuary, that is all. He watched as the coffins displayed their dead. He hid behind the stones as they buried them in the earth. He looked upon the deceiver who swore false vengeance.'

'Are you telling me that Thaddeus Myers didn't kill his family and hid in the church to escape his accusers?' asked Hettie, getting a little short on patience. 'How can you know that? Is it written down somewhere?'

Jacob smiled again. 'Perhaps it will come to pass. It is in the hands of the avenging angel. And now I must bid you farewell. My time is short and there is much to do.' Jacob turned from the ring of stones and began to walk slowly towards the church.

Hettie watched him go, then called after him. 'Wait! Who *is* the avenging angel?'

Jacob did not turn round, but his reply was borne clearly on the wind. 'You are.'

Hettie shivered. The cold of the churchyard was getting into her bones and her head was full of Jacob Surplus's riddles. She made her way back towards the main road, delighted to see that Bruiser, Tilly and Scarlet were waiting for her in the lay-by. Tilly was obviously bursting to tell her what she had discovered in the villages, but they decided to postpone an exchange of news until they were in front of a roaring fire.

On arriving home, Hettie made a beeline for her chair and remained there in silence while Tilly busied herself laying the table for supper and coaxing the fire back to life. Bruiser accepted a warming mug of tea and took himself off down the shed with his sausage pie and cream horn. Tilly could see that her friend was troubled. Hettie had shown no interest in the supper that sat untouched on the table, and Tilly sat quietly on her blanket by the fire, waiting for her to speak. It was some time before she was able to transfer her thoughts to words.

'It seems like someone's playing a huge game with us,' she began. 'I think this Milky Myers stuff is a smokescreen for what's really happening.' Hettie struggled from her chair and pulled Mavis's note from her mac pocket. 'Look at this. Mavis was obviously convinced that Lavinia was in some sort of danger, and then there's the will – she decided not to leave her house to Lavinia, yet she leaves enough money for Lavinia to buy a house anyway. And why leave the house in Whisker Terrace to Irene Peggledrip when she has a substantial home of her own? And what did Mavis Spitforce have against Bhaji Dosh? He seems a good, genuine sort, and he obviously loves Lavinia.'

Tilly listened carefully, jotting down the odd word here and there in her notebook and waiting for the right moment to offer the fruits of her own labours. 'What about the vicar at St Biscuit's?' she asked. 'Did he shed some light on anything?'

Hettie shivered at the memory. 'Well, it was all a bit weird. He appeared in the middle of that snowstorm, standing in front of the Myers' graves.'

'What snowstorm?' Tilly looked puzzled.

'The one this afternoon, almost on the dot of three o'clock. Anyway, he showed me the graves of all the Myers who were murdered in the original story and he seemed to know a lot about the case, but he's not one for a straight answer and I'm still trying to work out exactly what it was that he told me. I think the gist of it is that Thaddeus Myers was innocent and hid in the church to avoid being captured. I suspect from what Jacob said that Thaddeus knew who had killed his family; he probably witnessed the murder of his father and escaped before the same thing could happen to him. But none of that leads us to the present and the cat who killed Mavis and Teezle. My guess is that it's all to do with family secrets.'

It was time for Tilly to add her story, although she was rather disappointed not to able to include a snowstorm in the telling; there had been nothing more than a raw wind where she and Bruiser had ventured. She flicked through her notebook until she came to the right page, wanting to be as accurate with the details as possible.

'We started in Much-Purring-on-the-Cushion. Lily Slipper is buried there in St Savouries'. According to the old gravedigger, she was the village hairdresser and electrocuted herself by mistake under one of her hairdryers. Burnt to a crisp, by all accounts. Next came Osbert Tubbs. He had a very successful dairy in the High Street in Much-Purring-on-the-Step. He even had his own small herd of cows, which turned out to be unfortunate.'

'Why?' asked Hettie, having a very good idea of what was coming next.

'He was trampled to death by them early one morning after he'd finished milking. Not much left to bury, according to the vicar at St Whiskers'.' Tilly's account of the death toll around the villages – although tragic for those involved – was beginning to lift Hettie's spirits; in fact, she found herself stifling a snigger here and there as the list of catastrophes continued.

'Next came Hermione Bundle. She's got a lovely plot in St Bristles' in Much-Purring-on-the-Blanket. She was over a hundred when she died. She choked on a gobstopper and was found covered in sherbet behind her sweet counter. The whole village went into mourning for her. Now, Augustus Pump was a nasty one. He ran the local pub in Much-Purring-on-the-Mat.'

'Why was he nasty?' Hettie asked, beginning to get her appetite back.

'*He* wasn't nasty as far as I know; it's what happened

to him. He was in his yard directing the drays towards the beer cellar doors and . . .'

'He was trampled by the horses?'

'No. He was run over by the cart wheels and squashed into the cobbles. It took them ages to gather up the bits. Most of him is buried in St Mat's.' Even Tilly supressed a giggle at this point, and moved on to the final death on Mavis Spitforce's list. 'It was hard to find out much about Horace Winkle. He died some time ago, but it appears that he sold seafood from his front room when he could get hold of it. Much-Purring-on-the-Chair is the closest village to the sea besides Southwool, and Horace had connections with cats that fished along the coast. I spoke to an old cat who was sweeping up leaves in her garden, and she said Horace had a big fish tank in his front room – you could choose the fish you wanted while it was still swimming around. She said he'd been attacked by a shoal of jellyfish that were delivered by mistake. He turned bright orange and tripled in size, evidently. That's probably why he has such a big plot in the churchyard.'

Both Tilly and Hettie burst out into fits of uncontrollable laughter and it was some time before a certain amount of decorum was restored. Hettie rose from her chair, collected their sausage pies from the table, and carried them back to the fireside. 'Well, after all that, I'm suddenly starving.' They made short work of the pies and went straight back to the nuts and bolts of the case. There had been a number of breakthroughs, it seemed; it was just a matter of identifying them.

'Did you work out what the blue boxes were on the map?' asked Hettie, loading her pipe.

'They seem to mark the places where all those dead cats had shops or businesses. It's hard to tell exactly, as there are other shops there now. Osbert Tubbs' dairy is now a huge Dosh Store, and Augustus Pump's pub is an Indian takeaway with a Dosh shop next door.'

'There seems to be a Dosh Store round every corner of this case,' said Hettie, settling to her catnip. 'I wonder when the first branch of the family arrived from India? That family tree Mavis was working on didn't go back very far. I suppose it was a work in progress.'

'Maybe we should talk to Pakora, like Balti suggested. She's quite old, and she might know a bit more about her family's history.'

The thought of having to interview Pakora Dosh didn't fill Hettie with any warmth, but Tilly was right and a longer conversation with Rogan could also prove helpful. 'I think we'll leave the Doshes until Saturday, it being the perfect day for gunpowder, treason and plot,' she said, eyeing up the cream horns that sat unmolested on the table. 'I don't know why, but I think it's more important to get our meeting with

Irene Peggledrip out of the way first. I'm interested in why she seems to know so much about the times of death for Mavis and Teezle. I wonder if she knows that Mavis left her the house?'

'She should have seen it coming if she's a real psychic.'

'Mm. And we mustn't forget that she actually lives in the house where this whole sorry mess began. I think tomorrow will be a very interesting day. And now I suggest we relieve the table of those cream horns and put the milk on for the cocoa.'

CHAPTER ELEVEN

Friday dawned with a ringing in Hettie's ears. It persisted until Tilly had successfully negotiated the contents of the staff sideboard to locate the telephone, which rang rarely and only at the least convenient times. During business hours, it was Tilly's job as office junior to field any outside communications and to give the impression that the No. 2 Feline Detective Agency was a busy and efficient organisation. Today, with Hettie still swathed in her bed covers and Tilly in her winter pyjamas, the impression was a little far from the mark.

'Oh bugger!' exclaimed Tilly as she backed out of

the sideboard, bringing the telephone with her. 'That's just typical – it's stopped. You'd think it would have the decency to wait until I could answer it. It's plain bad manners to disturb us and then ring off.' She slammed the offending creature down next to her blanket and put the kettle on. The clock said five past eight and an early morning cup of milky tea might help to repair the jangling nerves of such a rude awakening.

Hettie, now fully awake, sat up. 'Why anyone would want to call at this time defeats me. Nobody decent would be awake enough to pick up the phone in the first place.'

'I suppose most cats are up by now if they have jobs to go to,' Tilly said reasonably, adding an extra sugar lump to her tea.

'Well, they should keep their early rising habits to themselves and not bother the rest of us with them.' Hettie was about to launch into one of her rants when the telephone rang again.

Tilly responded immediately, pulling the receiver off the hook. 'Good morning, the No. 2 Feline Detective Agency, Tilly Jenkins speaking – how may I help?' Hettie was impressed, and marvelled at what Tilly liked to call her 'posh voice'. The measured decorum was soon shattered and the caller was clearly in a hurry. 'Oh, just a minute Miss Anderton – I'll see if Miss Bagshot is able to take your call.' Tilly covered the mouthpiece with her paw. 'It's Bugs Anderton. She sounds very upset. I think you'll have to speak to her.'

Grudgingly, Hettie took the proffered phone. 'Miss Anderton, what can I do for you?' It was several moments before she was able to get another word in, but eventually she gained control of the conversation. 'We have arranged a meeting with Miss Peggledrip today, but we could come and see you tomorrow to discuss this properly if that would help? We have other business in Much-Purring, so shall we say two o'clock?'

Having finalised the appointment, Hettie passed the phone back to Tilly, who in turn pushed it back into the staff sideboard. 'Whatever's the matter with her? I thought there'd been another murder by the way she was shrieking down the phone.'

'Not yet,' Hettie said wryly, giving the fire a good poke. 'She's had a nasty threatening note saying that if she doesn't clear off back to Scotland she'll be sharing a plot with her friend Mavis. Evidently there have been some odd things happening in her garden recently, as well – broken panes in her greenhouse, paint sprayed on her rose garden, and bags of rubbish appearing from nowhere. On the face of it, it doesn't seem very serious, but coupled with the threatening note and the fact that it all sounds very similar to the problems Mavis was having a few weeks ago, I think we should look into it. We have to pay a call on Pakora Dosh tomorrow anyway, so we'll kill two birds with one stone. Today we enter the weird and wonderful world of Irene Peggledrip and her friend Crimola.'

Tilly clapped her paws in excitement. She had been looking forward to visiting the town's medium all week, and sprang to the filing cabinet to select the garment that she thought would be most suitable for the day's adventure. After much pondering over which colour would best suit her first foray into the spirit world, and a complete fashion parade in front of a disinterested Hettie, she decided on the purple cardigan with hood and bright yellow buttons – the one she had picked out right from the start. Several rounds of toast and cheese triangles later, she tidied their room whilst Hettie strode off down the garden to wake Bruiser, only to find him in deep conversation with Beryl Butter about her plans for the bonfire night celebrations the next day. Hettie had already stepped forward as chief firework warden and would be giving her display, assisted by Tilly as torch bearer and carrier of matches. Bruiser, it would appear, was being coerced into taking charge of the bonfire in exchange for as many sausage rolls as he could eat.

Satisfied that her new recruit was on board, Beryl bustled back up the garden to help her sister with the breakfast rush in the shop. Hettie helped Bruiser throw some more wood onto the bonfire, which was beginning to look impressive.

'This'll go up a treat tomorrow, as long as we don't

have any rain,' he said, pleased to be part of the party. 'What yer got in store fer us today?'

Hettie took a moment to respond as she picked a splinter out of her paw. 'Nice things this morning, odd stuff this afternoon. We have to go to Hambone's to pick up the fireworks for tomorrow, that's the first job; then lunch and off to the Peggledrip house for God knows what this afternoon. If you don't fancy staying, you can drop us off and pick us up later.'

Bruiser appreciated Hettie's diplomacy but was quite enjoying his role as bodyguard. 'No, I'll wait fer yer. Yer might need a quick getaway from there.' Strangely, Bruiser was right.

Tilly was waiting excitedly when Hettie got back to their room. 'Look – Betty's dropped off the money for the fireworks. She said they've raised twice as much as last year by putting an extra penny on their Halloween novelties.'

'We'd better get a move on, then, if you're going to choose them this year. It's a big responsibility.'

She waited for the words to register with her friend, and wasn't disappointed. 'Me? Do you mean me to choose the fireworks?' Tilly squealed, forgetting her arthritis and dancing round the room. She swung the bag of money about so vigorously that she collapsed in a fluffy heap on Hettie's giant red bean bag, unseating the twelve-string guitar which Hettie only just caught before it crashed to the floor.

Hettie laughed at the sheer joy on Tilly's face. 'Come on. Bruiser will be waiting for us. We'll let Meridian Hambone count the money while you pick out your display.'

Bruiser was posting the end of one of the Butters' finest sausage rolls into his mouth when Hettie and Tilly joined him in the High Street. It occurred to Hettie that he was becoming quite a hit with the sisters, who were obviously enjoying having a strong pair of male paws about the place. He had certainly settled into his position at the No. 2 Feline Detective Agency, and Hettie's fear of having to drive the motorbike quite slipped away from her as she and Tilly settled into Scarlet's sidecar to be chauffeured to Hambone's in the style to which they had both become accustomed.

Meridian Hambone squawked with delight as Tilly swung the firework money onto her counter. 'Gawd love us! This'll buy yer plenty of whoops and bangs, and I got 'em on specials today – four fireworks gets yer a free pack o' me sparklers.'

Tilly clapped her paws in delight. She loved watching the fireworks as they exploded into showers of gold and silver in the bonfire night sky, but sparklers were her ultimate joy and the anticipation of writing her name with a fizzing stick of magical sparks was almost too much to look forward to. Hettie collected a wire shopping basket and stood patiently whilst she debated over how to strike the perfect balance between spectacular, pretty and just plain noisy. 'I think I'll do the ones on the floor first,' she said, to no one in particular. 'Golden Rain, that's a nice one, and Roman Candles – four of those. The pyramiddy things look exciting – I think four of those as well.'

Hettie loaded the basket as Tilly worked her way through the 'pretty' part of her choices, moving on to what she liked to call 'the tricky ones'. 'I suppose we'd better have some Jumping Jacks, although I got chased by one last year and it made me drop my toffee apple. Then there was the Catherine Wheel incident.' Hettie nodded sagely, remembering the moment when the spinning firework had detached itself from the fence to which she had nailed it and completed its colourful swirling in Lavender Stamp's newly knitted cloche hat, much to Lavender's surprise and the delight of those who had been made to stand a little too long in one of her queues. Thinking aloud, Tilly continued. 'But it wouldn't be the same without the Catherine Wheels, so I think eight of those and four Jumping Jacks and four of those Aeroplanes.'

The basket was now full of colourful tubes of gunpowder of every shape and size, and Tilly reached the 'spectacular' section of her display – the rockets. Much to the annoyance of Creamy Float the milk-cat, Tilly had been hoarding empty bottles for several weeks to ensure that the Butters' rocket display would be a magnificent spectacle; it was traditionally saved until the end of the firework display, just before the lighting of the bonfire. Now, the rockets stood on their sticks like soldiers across the back of the display cabinet, starting with the smaller ones and building to the giant spaceship shapes with cardboard fins and wings. Remembering the deal on the sparklers, Tilly selected four of each size, giving her twenty-four rockets in total.

Hettie staggered to the counter under the weight of Tilly's choices, just as Meridian had finished counting the firework money. 'Near as damn it, twenty pounds there. Old Guy Fawkes'd be pleased to 'ave that much gunpowder!' she squawked as she began adding up the contents of Hettie's basket. Eventually, after several recounts and much crossing out on the notepad she kept by the till, Meridian was able to give the financial statement that Hettie and Tilly had been waiting for. 'I makes that nineteen pound and threepence, with twelve free packs of sparklers.' Hettie was pleased that Tilly's extravagance hadn't broken the bank, and Tilly was ecstatic at having achieved so many packets of free sparklers. It was going to be a very fine display.

Bruiser sauntered through from the yard with a borrowed copy of *Biker's Monthly* under his arm, just in time to carry the fireworks in several large brown paper bags. They fitted nicely into the sidecar but there was no room for Hettie or Tilly, so it was agreed that Bruiser would run the fireworks home whilst the other two picked up fish and chips for lunch. Hettie had pointed out that they may need a hearty meal to sustain them during their afternoon at the Peggledrip house, and she received no argument from either Tilly or Bruiser.

Elsie Haddock's Fish Emporium was almost as popular as the Butters' pie and pastry shop. From opposite ends of the High Street, they served the townsfolk with premium quality foods and service. Elsie had been in fish all her life, and had jealously guarded a family recipe for crispy batter which brought cats from as far away as Southwool to dine – on or off the premises. 'Dining in' consisted of two small tables placed by the salt and vinegar shelf where, on cold and rainy days if you were lucky, you could sit and eat in the warm. Today, there was no chance: the shop was packed to the gills, as it always was on a Friday, and the tables had been pushed to one side to allow more space for the queue of salivating customers. Elsie stood at the helm of her empire, as broad as she was tall and swathed in chef's battered and splattered whites, wielding her frying baskets with a precision to be gasped at. There was a remarkable intimacy between Elsie and her deep fat fryers, and even though her days were long and tiring, she had never entertained the prospect of taking on staff; in her darkest moments, she allowed the thought of another cat tampering with her built-in heat regulators to enter her charmed life, but mostly those unthinkable demons were kept at bay. She had also fought off the developing trend of menu expansion, sticking strictly to a choice of cod, her namesake Haddock, and the option of small or large chips; she had given in to the idea of homemade fish cakes, which were popular with kittens, but there was no chance of finding a pie or a saveloy anywhere on the premises.

In spite of its being a one-cat show, the queue moved swiftly. Hettie's hunger reached fever pitch as the smell of freshly fried fish and chips engulfed her, and she eyed the newspaper parcels of successful customers with murderous intent as they swaggered out of the shop. At last, her turn came and she boldly delivered her request of cod and large chips, three times. Tilly stood poised at the salt and vinegar bar to add the condiments as Elsie slapped the still-sizzling cod and three generous shovels of chips into the middle of a sheet of newspaper. By coincidence, the paper was the edition of the *Sunday Snout* which carried the details of their triumphant Furcross case; Tilly hesitated to pour vinegar all over the picture of Hettie, but pushed on in the knowledge that they had several copies somewhere at home.

Armed with their precious cargo, they skipped from the fish shop and made short work of their walk home, where it would be true to say that Elsie Haddock's fish and chips were despatched in less time than it took to boil a kettle.

194

'Well, we can't put Irene Peggledrip off any longer,' sighed Hettie after a long and intense cleaning of paws and whiskers. 'I'll pop round and order pies for supper and meet you both by Scarlet.' Hettie pulled her business mac from its hook and grabbed her warmest scarf; she left by the back door, only to return seconds later agitated and annoyed. 'We won't be going anywhere just yet. The alleyway is blocked. And you'll never guess what's bloody blocking it?'

Tilly exchanged a nervous look with Bruiser, who leapt into action. 'Well, whatever it is I'll fix it!'

Hettie and Tilly followed him out into the yard and the three cats peered down the alleyway that led to the High Street as a giant woolly monster scraped and shoved its way towards them. Tilly shrank back behind Hettie as Bruiser prepared for battle. 'Come on!' he shouted. 'All paws on deck. Let's shove it back before it gets into the yard.' He flung himself at the obstruction which was making very good progress along the passage, and Hettie and Tilly added their weight to his charge. The monster rebuffed them all by bouncing Bruiser backwards and creating a painful pile-up of claws and fur.

It was, in fact, Betty Butter who saved the day. Hearing the commotion as she placed a tray of bonfire buns in the bread oven, she bustled into the yard in time to stop Bruiser's second assault on the monster. 'Eee, there's nowt ta be fearful of. It's Lavender Stamp's Mr

Fawkes for the bonfire – 'e's a beauty this year, she's done us proud.' No sooner had Betty explained than all became clear. The giant hand-knitted Guy Fawkes popped out of the alleyway and unfolded itself to its full glory, hotly pursued by Beryl Butter and Lavender Stamp, who had collectively given their stuffed hero the extra-large push required to finish the job.

Lavender was no stranger to knitted dolls. It was something she'd taken up many years ago after being jilted by Laxton Sprat, a rather handsome post-cat who had treated her badly and given her a nasty dose of fleas. Lavender's mother, who ran the Post Office at the time, encouraged her daughter to take up knitting as therapy to help her get over her disappointment. Since then, Lavender had become obsessed with knitting male cats of every shape and size, creating her ideal companion out of wool and shunning any close contact with the real thing. The dolls were perfect in every detail, and Lavender shared her fireside with them during the long winter evenings. Those that turned out to be less successful were abandoned to a glass case in the Post Office and bore extortionate price tags; they were rarely sold, but gave Lavender's customers something to focus on during the long haul to the counter. The fact that Laxton Sprat had caused all the trouble in the first place went a long way to explaining the animosity Lavender showed towards Laxton's sister, Marmite; not only did she refuse to stock her 'little books' in the Post Office, but she had gone as far as to advise her not to darken the counter at all. Laxton Sprat had gone on to become a film director, getting an international reputation for dubious shorts; he rarely returned to the town, which was, as far as Lavender was concerned, a blessing.

Tilly looked up at the Guy in wonder. Now he was unfolded, she could admire his colourful clothes – his bright red jacket, royal blue trousers, and green shoes with golden buckles. 'Oh, he's lovely! It's such a shame to put him on the bonfire.' As if he were listening, the Guy nodded his head in tune with a gust of wind.

Hettie looked up at the sky. 'It looks like rain. If Mr Fawkes gets wet, he won't burn at all.'

Beryl agreed, and it was decided that an attempt should be made to wrestle the Guy into the hallway next to the bread ovens. Having delivered her prize, Lavender beat a hasty retreat back to the Post Office and Betty returned to the shop to deal with the lunchtime stragglers, leaving Beryl, Hettie, Tilly and Bruiser to wrestle the giant knit through the back door. There were several difficult moments before he was finally propped up in a sitting position next to the bread ovens; at one point, Beryl became wedged in the arms of Mr Fawkes in the doorway, and had it not been for Bruiser's swift action, she might have been suffocated before the task was complete.

The four cats, ruffled and out of breath,

congratulated themselves on a job well done. To celebrate, Beryl rescued the bonfire buns from the oven and handed them round just as there was a knock on the back door. Burning her paws on the hot bun, Hettie threw the door open to be confronted by a pile of newly stained wood and a round jovial cat with a delivery note. 'Delivery from Prunes and Pots for Miss Butter,' he said, forcing the note into Hettie's paw.

Flushed from the oven, Beryl came forward. 'Ah, Mr Prune! Thank you for fitting me in. Could you leave it down at the bottom of the garden?' Mr Prune looked a little put out, knowing that his garden centre lorry was blocking the High Street, but the Butter sisters were good customers and deserved to be treated well. Bruiser took charge of the delivery and helped carry the assorted shapes and sizes of wood to the bottom of the garden while Hettie and Tilly made short work of the bonfire buns and reserved three steak and ale pies for supper, which Beryl promised to leave on their doorstep if they were late home.

CHAPTER TWELVE

The November fog was already forming by the time they reached the Peggledrip house. The earlier brightness of the day was gone, replaced by a dull, murky mist of fine rain. The old house stood like some long-forgotten mansion, lifeless and unwelcoming. Hettie sat for a moment staring up at it from the comfort of Scarlet's sidecar, trying to imagine the day when a whole family had been slaughtered there with such violence. She wondered how much that had affected the house. Did death linger once the physical remains had been cleared away? Did the dead accept their lot, or did they return to inhabit a world which was happy to move on without them? Suddenly, she remembered what it was that had been nagging at her for days. 'That's it!' she exclaimed, pulling the sidecar lid open and making Tilly jump. 'Rogan Dosh! He was coming out of the driveway in his van. Bruiser had to swerve to miss him.'

Tilly cottoned on quickly. 'Yes, that's right. It was the day we found poor Teezle in the tree.'

'Exactly!' shouted Hettie, triumphantly helping Tilly out onto the driveway. 'You'd need a van to shift a body, especially one the size of Teezle Makepeace. Come on! Let's find out what Irene Peggledrip has to say for herself.'

Bruiser took their place in Scarlet's sidecar, settling down with his magazine and a tartan rug to keep out the chill, while Hettie and Tilly climbed the steps to the front door. Hettie was about to lift the door knocker, which grimaced at her in a Marleyesque way, when the still air was permeated by a put-put coming down the driveway. Turning round in surprise, she witnessed the arrival of a pink scooter. The rider, complete with peaked skid lid, ballooned out with the force of the wind in her all-weather Pac a Mac, and applied her brakes just in time to miss taking out the rose border which fronted the house. Climbing off the machine, she rocked the vehicle back on its stabilisers and proceeded to divest herself of the scooter helmet which had so far concealed her identity.

'Good grief!' said Hettie, just loud enough for Tilly to hear. 'It's Beverages and Embroidered Kneelers.'

Tilly giggled as Delirium Treemints puffed her way up the steps to join them. 'Oh Miss Bagshot, thank goodness you have only just arrived. Miss Peggledrip has engaged me on refreshments for the afternoon, and due to a slight mishap with Susie Cooper, I was running a bit late.'

Hettie smiled out of sympathy for the cat called Susie Cooper, not realising that Delirium was referring to a pale green tea service that had decided to leap off her kitchen dresser before she left home, delaying her as she swept up the broken pottery. Delirium collected pottery, which was just as well bearing in mind how often she broke it, and replacements were always welcome.

The door knocker received a mighty swing and Hettie was rewarded within seconds by the sound of a key being turned in the lock and a shooting back of bolts. The door opened to reveal Irene Peggledrip, clad in a long druid-like purple robe embellished with tiny circles of mirror glass and tied at the waist with a golden tasselled rope. To complete the necromantic effect, she wore a pair of curious slippers, bright yellow and turned up at the toes as if doubling back on themselves. Hettie resisted the hysterical laughter which rose in her throat, quickly disguising it as a cough, and Tilly stared in awe at the magical vision before her, pleased to have chosen the 'in house' colour for her cardigan.

Having achieved the desired effect, Irene Peggledrip welcomed her guests. 'My dears, please come in out of the cold. How lovely to see you! Delirium, perhaps you could make your way through to the kitchen and prepare the afternoon tea. We're using the melamine set to avoid breakages.'

Delirium looked relieved and blew down the hallway, disappearing into the back of the house and leaving Irene to entertain her guests. 'Crimola will be joining us a little later in the parlour. Perhaps you'd like to come through to the library first? I have a lovely fire on the go in there and we can have a nice chat. Leave your coats on the pegs by the door.'

Hettie and Tilly removed their business macs but left their scarves on to look a little more dressed up and colourful for the occasion. They followed their host into a high ceilinged room with walls completely covered in books from top to bottom. A large fireplace was the only relief from the tomes, but even there the mantelpiece acted as an extra shelf. Tilly gasped in admiration at the different coloured spines, noting the wooden ladder on which a reader might glide up and down to her heart's content, selecting and savouring the books on offer. She had seen the town's chief librarian, Turner Page, shoot along the shelves on such a ladder in the old library before they closed it to build a car park.

Hettie, who took very little interest in books, made a beeline for the fire and – at Irene's invitation – settled herself in one of the leather armchairs close to the grate. Irene took the one opposite and Tilly sat between them on a small leather patchwork pouffe, decorated with elephants. She pulled her notebook from her cardigan pocket and waited for Hettie to begin her interrogation.

Surprisingly, it was Irene Peggledrip who asked the first few questions. 'Miss Bagshot, are you any closer to finding the cat who murdered my dear friend Mavis?'

Hettie responded with the official line. 'We have a number of strong suspects, and I'm convinced that the perpetrator will be revealed very soon.'

'And what about that poor girl in my tree? Is she connected to Mavis's death?'

Hettie felt able to answer this question in a more positive way. 'I'm pleased that you've raised the issue of Teezle Makepeace. You see, the day we found her hanging from your tree was also the day that Rogan Dosh was seen coming out of your driveway in his van.'

Irene thought for a moment. 'Well, that must have been on Wednesday – it's my Indian curry night. First it's backgammon with Crimola, then a lovely hot bath with essence of Amritsar, followed by one of Rogan and Balti's TV suppers. I'm working my way through a boxed set of Bollywood greats at the moment. Of course, I didn't get as far as the bath or the supper this week. I just didn't have the heart after seeing that poor girl strung up in such a way.'

'How do you receive your delivery from Rogan Dosh?' asked Hettie. 'Does he come to the front door or round the back?'

'To the back door, of course. He parks his van at the side and knocks on the kitchen window – unless I'm out, in which case he leaves it all in the old dairy. But I was in on Wednesday when he came. He made me jump actually when he banged on the window. I hadn't heard the van, you see. He was in a terrible hurry and wouldn't stop for a cup of tea – he said he had some deliveries for his Aunt Pakora, and she doesn't take prisoners.'

'After the delivery, did you go out into the garden for any reason?'

'No, it was a miserable day. I didn't set foot out of the house until your friend here fetched me to come and see the body.'

'So if Rogan had brought the body with him and strung it up in your tree, you wouldn't have noticed?' Hettie clarified, pressing home her point.

Irene Peggledrip was visibly shocked at the suggestion and stared down at her yellow Turkish slippers for several moments, deciding what to say next. As if a decision had arrived from nowhere, she rose from her chair and left the room, leaving Hettie and Tilly without a word of explanation. 'Maybe Crimola has arrived,' offered Tilly as her eyes did another appraisal of the bookshelves.

'Who can say? But I think we had her rattled over the Rogan Dosh thing. She knows a lot more than she's saying.'

Irene Peggledrip returned to the library in time to hear the end of Hettie's sentence and joined in the conversation. 'You're absolutely right, of course – there *are* things I must tell you, secrets that are now covering up the truth. Like this, for instance.' Irene held up a long piece of wire. 'Cheese! You see?'

Hettie and Tilly exchanged a look that confirmed they were both ready to leave in a hurry if necessary. Irene, seeing that she had alarmed them, returned to her chair by the fire and placed the wire in Hettie's paws. 'I took this from around that poor girl's neck before Shroud and Trestle removed her from the dairy. As you quite rightly said, she was strangled with it – but look at it more closely, and smell it.'

Hettie did as she was told, and had to agree that the wire carried a faint odour of cheese. 'I'm sorry, Miss Peggledrip, but what are you saying? What has cheese got to do with it?'

Irene opened her mouth to respond, but it was Tilly who spoke first. 'I've got it! It's a cheese wire. Rogan Dosh uses one all the time in his shop for cutting cheese!'

Irene nodded her approval in Tilly's direction and Hettie looked more closely at the wire before responding 'Why did you decide to remove the wire from Teezle's neck?'

'It was Crimola. She was being spiteful over the backgammon, and after I'd won she flounced out of my head shouting "check the girl's neck if you want to catch a murderer".'

'She actually said that to you?'

'Oh yes, that's what she's like when she's cross. She shows off, you see – tells me things I didn't know and clears off without giving me any opportunity for clarification.'

Hettie was still having problems with the concept of Crimola. The evidence was beginning to build against Rogan Dosh, but why would he kill Teezle Makepeace? And then there was Mavis – what had she done to be killed in such a way? There was the issue of Bhaji and Lavinia, but murder seemed an extreme solution to that sort of problem. Hettie was determined to glean as much information as possible from Irene Peggledrip and decided to go right back to the beginning. 'Miss Peggledrip, you say there are secrets which are covering up the truth – are they related to Mavis Spitforce?'

Irene smiled. 'Well done you. Yes, Mavis shared a number of secrets with me. We were very close. She never acknowledged our friendship in public because of my "gifts", as she called them. You see, Mavis digested knowledge like you and I would eat a cream cake. We shared this library; all her factual books are on that wall there, and my "off colour philosophies", as she put it, are on the opposite wall over there. We agreed to share the library when I bought the house from her years ago. It was the only room she couldn't bear to part with.'

Tilly was making furious notes as Hettie interrupted the Peggledrip flow. 'You say you bought the house from Mavis? I thought the place was derelict before you took it over.'

'Abandoned and unloved is closer to the mark,' Irene continued. 'You see, Mavis had inherited the place from her father, Merry Spitforce. He'd never lived here – none of the family returned after the Myers murders, and the house was just handed down the generations like a rope around their necks. They all lived in the shadow of Thaddeus Myers' guilt, and the house stood as a reminder to the terrible crimes committed here.'

'So why didn't the family get rid of it straight away after the murders?' asked Hettie.

'Because of the gossip. Folk thought that "Milky" was still at large and would murder anyone who came near the place, so the house carried a curse round here and was to be avoided at all costs. No one showed any interest in buying it, except at the beginning.'

Hettie looked up from the fire. 'What do you mean?'

'The story goes that shortly after the murders, the cat who owned the village stores in Much-Purring-on-the-Rug – who, incidentally, discovered the bodies – tried to buy the place off a distant Myers relative, but for some reason he backed out at the last minute.'

Hettie suddenly recalled her last conversation with Jacob Surplus, and especially the bit about hiding in the church and watching the killer as he took part in the Myers family's funeral. 'Do you know the name of the cat from Much-Purring?'

'I do now. Mavis found out just before she died. She'd been doing a family tree for Balti and it turned out to be Rogan's great-great-grandfather, Jalfrezi. According to Mavis, he'd recently arrived from India bringing his family with him, and had used the family fortune to set up the very first convenience stores. His plan was to knock this house down and build a delivery depot to supply his shops. He was going to keep the dairy at the back, as it was a very successful business in the Myers' time. The odd thing was that after the house fell through Jalfrezi went back to India, abandoning his family who appeared to blossom and flourish very well without him. In fact, I don't know what we'd do these days without a Dosh Stores in every town and village.'

Hettie was sorely tempted to say 'survive', but she resisted the sarcasm in favour of another question.

'Why did Mavis Spitforce finally decide to sell the house to you?'

'That's an easy one. I'd met her on a rambling holiday. It was terrible, actually – wind and rain non-stop for two weeks, up in the Highlands somewhere. Anyway, I would entertain with my readings in the evenings at the hostel where we all stayed.'

'Readings? What do you mean?'

'Oh my dear, I'm sorry – my knowings is what I should have said. I used to do it with the gravy left on plates. I could see shapes and then odd things would come into my head – warnings, that sort of thing. Mavis was very sceptical until one night I saw the outline of this house on her plate. It was all there in the gravy, and I told her before she could protest.'

Tilly leant forward, not wanting the story to end and having quite forgotten to take notes for some time. Hettie, at the mention of gravy, was half-heartedly wondering what Delirium Treemints was preparing in the kitchen, but she asked the question expected of her. 'And what did you see in her gravy?'

'I saw a dark cloud over the house, a box of gold coins, and talking milk bottles.'

Hettie was trying to imagine Mavis Spitforce's reactions to the contents of her plate and decided to encourage further enlightenment. 'So what was your interpretation of what you saw?'

'That wasn't for me to say. I only say what I see – the

interpretation is up to the cat who owns the gravy, and I can tell you that Mavis was shocked at what I'd said. She went on to tell me about the house and its past and what a burden it was to her. At the time, she even believed the Milky Myers story and she told me how ashamed she was to have a murderer in her family. I could see that she needed to be rid of the house so I offered to buy it – ghosts, murderers and all. I was looking for a new start after a rather unfortunate run-in with the Knock Three Times Society, charlatans, all of 'em.'

Hettie supressed a grin which threatened to take over her face and returned to the portents of the gravy. 'You mentioned a box of gold coins?'

'Ah, yes. I was spot on there. We found them several years ago behind a bound set of Agatha Crispys. Over there, as a matter of fact.' Irene pointed to a section of shelves dedicated to rare volumes of crime fiction. 'They were sovereigns, very valuable these days. Mavis was going to give them to her sister, Mildred, to make up for, er . . .'

'Taking her daughter away from her?' asked Hettie, finishing the sentence.

'Oh, I see you're aware of the skeletons in the cupboard. Poor Mildred, she just couldn't cope with Lavinia and the other company she kept. Not at all suitable to bring a kitten up surrounded by a bunch of toms. She had no idea who the father was, you know.'

Hettie refused to take part in a discussion on Lavinia's moral welfare and pushed on with another question. 'Miss Spitforce made a new will before she died. Were you aware of its contents?'

'Yes I was. She asked me if I would take on her house in Whisker Terrace. She didn't want Lavinia to have it because she thought that young Bhaji Dosh might wrestle it off her and set up an extension to his parents' shop next door. I think Rogan had offered her money for the house some time ago, but Mavis refused to sell. She asked me to rent the house out and put the money by for a rainy day in case Mildred or Lavinia ever needed anything. If push came to shove, I was to sell the house and invest the money for them. She made me promise not to sell to a Dosh, though, in light of her suspicions over Jalfrezi.'

'And what did she suspect?'

'Mavis appreciated that the Myers murders happened longer ago than anyone could remember. She did, however, believe that it was Jalfrezi Dosh who had murdered her family to try and get his paws on their business and the property. She also thought that he had murdered Thaddeus Myers as well, but after tracing the family history she realised that she was directly descended from him so he must have survived. She also told me that history was repeating itself and that's why she made a new will – to protect her family.'

'So Jacob Surplus was right.'

'Jacob?' said Irene. 'You're in touch with Jacob? Now that *is* impressive.'

'Why do you say that? He may be a little strange but he gave me a tour of the Myers' graves. He seemed to think I was some sort of avenging angel.'

'Well, he should know – he's been living with the angels these past fifty years,' said Irene, laughing as she spoke.

'Don't you mean out with the fairies?' countered Hettie, joining in on a joke that was about to backfire all over her.

'You've lost me now,' said Irene, looking puzzled. 'Jacob Surplus lives on a much higher plane than the rest of us. He's the very top layer of spirit world, and only appears to those who are able to interpret his wisdom.'

Hettie could feel the red flush which started at her whiskers and progressed rapidly to the tips of her ears. 'Are you telling me that Jacob Surplus is dead and that I have seen and spoken at length to a ghost?'

Irene nodded with satisfaction. 'That's exactly what I'm telling you, and you're in good company because he appeared to Mavis a few weeks ago as well. He told her to prepare herself for her journey. That's why she made the new will – she knew her time was short.'

Hettie was now frantically trying to remember if the graveyard cat had given her a similar warning of doom, but satisfied herself that an avenging angel could do very little on the 'other side'; remaining earthbound seemed to be her immediate future. 'Just a minute, Tilly – you saw him, didn't you? He met us by the church. He made you giggle.'

'I didn't see anyone. You're always talking to yourself and it makes me laugh. I just thought you were having one of your silly moments. I know you met him in the churchyard because you told me about it, but I never actually saw him.'

Hettie was beginning to feel embarrassed and a bit cross; even Tilly had withdrawn her support. She tried again, if only for her own sanity. 'I'm sure he wasn't a ghost. He made an appointment to meet me in the graveyard and he was there waiting after the snowstorm. He told me how Thaddeus had hidden in the church.'

'Snowstorm!' cried Irene Peggledrip. 'You lucky thing! Most mediums would give their right arm for a materialisation in a snowstorm. It shows he comes from the highest order to pull that one. And he told you about Thaddeus because he was there in his time – the Reverend Jacob Surplus was the vicar of St Biscuit's at the time of the Myers murders. If you go round to the back of the church you'll see his grave. Yes, yes, Crimola – I know you're there but you'll have to wait. We haven't had our tea yet, and Miss Bagshot is in shock.'

On cue, the library door was kicked open to reveal a shaking tray full of cups and saucers, a teapot, and a large plate of freshly baked scones oozing with jam and fresh cream. Tilly leapt up to help steady the tray's progress across the room to a small occasional table, where Delirium finally brought it into safe harbour.

'Thank you, Delirium. Will you be joining us for tea?' Irene admired the scones. 'I'm not sure if Miss Bagshot and her friend would be happy for you to sit in on the session today. I fear there are sensitive issues to discuss with Crimola. What's that you say? Yes, I know you're keen to get on but forcing your way into teatime isn't going to help, is it Crimola, dear?'

Hettie was beginning to feel as impatient as Crimola to 'get on'; still shocked by the Jacob Surplus revelation, she was also developing an urgent concern for Bugs Anderton. The net was tightening around Rogan Dosh and taking tea with Delirium Treemints, Irene Peggledrip and Crimola while he was still at large was not getting the job done. The evidence was stacking up, and the last thing she wanted to do was to squander the rest of the afternoon in one of Irene Peggledrip's weird séances. As it turned out, Hettie was absolutely right and three miles down the road all hell was about to break loose.

'What do you think, Miss Bagshot?' said Irene, forcing a large scone into Hettie's paws.

'I'm sorry, I was miles away,' said Hettie, trying to look interested. 'About what?'

Irene sighed. 'Would you be happy for Delirium to sit in? I've taken her on as my first protégée. She's learning fast, and her out of body stuff is coming on a treat. Isn't it Delirium, dear?'

Delirium beamed like a cat who rarely received compliments of any sort and made a good effort at pouring the tea into four cups with very little spillage. Looking across at her, Hettie felt that any form of rejection would be unkind. 'I have no objections to Miss Treemints joining us, as long as she can be trusted to be discreet should Crimola have any news.' Hettie could hardly believe that she had accepted Crimola's existence to the extent that she was including her as another cat in the room rather than one who lived in Irene Peggledrip's imagination; as it turned out, Crimola was about to save the day.

The scones were demolished in record time. Tilly managed two of them and was wiping her paw round her empty plate as Irene Peggledrip rose from her chair in a very strange manner and walked with slow, deliberate movements towards the door. Delirium responded immediately by dropping her cup and saucer on the floor, causing no damage whatsoever to the melamine. She picked the cup and saucer up and addressed Hettie and Tilly in hushed tones. 'Crimola is with us. She's in the parlour. I think we should go through.'

Hettie stood up and followed Delirium out of the room, hardly noticing that Tilly had caught hold of her paw for reassurance. The parlour was dark and heavy, and material drapes, Persian carpets and tasselled lampshades suppressed the small amount of light that leaked from two ornate table lamps. The décor reminded Tilly of her friend Jessie's sitting room at the back of her shop, but this room lacked Jessie's sense of comfort and wellbeing; the presence of Irene Peggledrip seated at the head of an oak carved refectory table gave the room an air of Gothic horror.

Delirium offered chairs to Hettie and Tilly, placing them either side of their host. She lit a candle and placed it in front of Irene's face, completing the other-worldly look, then sat down at the opposite end of the table to observe. Hettie looked across at Tilly, who gave a very slight shrug of the shoulders, and then the voice began. It was clearly coming from Irene Peggledrip because her mouth was slightly open, but her lips didn't move and the overall effect was that of a rather bad ventriloquist. The mirror glass on her gown twinkled in the candlelight, throwing out dancing circles of light around the room, and Tilly was transfixed. Hettie seethed at such a display of nonsense, but was impressed with the voice and decided to humour the situation for a little longer.

'I am Crimola, here to answer your questions,' the voice began in a low monotone. 'What do you seek?'

Hettie was keen to get it over with and plunged straight in. 'I want to know who murdered Mavis Spitforce and Teezle Makepeace.'

Crimola laughed. 'That is for you to decide.'

Hettie tried a different question. 'Did Rogan Dosh kill them?'

'No,' came the answer, much to Hettie's annoyance.

'Is there anything you can tell me that might help me find the killer?' begged Hettie, feeling stupid and a little desperate.

'I will tell you what I see. Three wheels, a bolt of orange silk, broken glass, a chart with many names, a thistle and another death, perhaps.'

Hettie stood up, knocking the candle over, and Tilly extinguished the flame with her sizeable paw. The hot wax splashed Irene Peggledrip, who collapsed in a bout of violent sneezing. The scene was chaos as Delirium Treemints ran to Irene's aid waving a handkerchief. Hettie grabbed Tilly by the cardigan and dragged her out into the hall. 'Come on! We may be too late already. Get your coat!' Tilly did as she was told. Hettie negotiated the bolts on the front door and flung it open as Irene Peggledrip and Delirium Treemints followed on in hot pursuit from the abandoned parlour. Hettie cleared the steps with one impressive leap, injuring her foot slightly, and hammered on the lid to Scarlet's sidecar, where Bruiser had dozed off. 'Quick! Get the engine running – we're off to Much-Purring. It's an emergency!'

Bruiser struggled out of the sidecar, wiping the sleep from his eyes. Hettie bounced Tilly into her seat, throwing their business macs on top, and settled in beside her.

'Wait for me!' screamed Irene Peggledrip, falling down her own steps and trying to cram her Cossack hat onto her head as her trench coat blew out behind her. With a bound she installed herself on the back of the motorbike, much to Bruiser's surprise. Delirium – having pulled on her Pac a Mac and skid lid – was left in a puff of Scarlet's smoke to start up her scooter and follow on behind, while the door to the Peggledrip house stood wide open, revealing the ghosts of the Myers family huddled in the doorway, watchful and smiling.

Bruiser gave Scarlet full throttle, skilfully avoiding two farm tractors and a bin lorry, but collecting a number of branches and brambles from the hedgerows which fixed themselves to Irene's hat. Delirium had not been so lucky with the bin lorry and had applied her brakes slightly too late to avoid the backdraught of the town's meat and veg rubbish; not until the next day did she discover a rancid pork chop lodged in her rear wheel arch. Tilly and Hettie hung on inside the sidecar, wishing that they had avoided the cream scones; soon, their flight was over and Bruiser brought Scarlet to a standstill outside the Dosh Stores.

The door was open and the shop looked deserted, which was strange for a Friday afternoon. The vegetable stands had been abandoned with not even an honesty box in sight, but the screaming could be heard as soon as Hettie pulled back the roof on the sidecar. She sprang into action, racing down Bugs Anderton's path next to the store, followed closely by Tilly, Irene and eventually Delirium Treemints. Bruiser, noticing a trail of blood leading from the Dosh Stores, went inside to investigate, making his way through to Pakora's kitchen.

Bugs's front door was wide open and the screaming had stopped. As Hettie moved cautiously over the threshold, her heart sank. It was too late: the cream carpet and beige wallpaper were covered in blood. She advanced her party towards the sitting room where they had taken tea only recently; there, lying on the floor, was the body of Bugs Anderton in a sickening red pool. Hettie crossed to the body as the other three cats looked on from the doorway. Suddenly, her hackles rose as a flurry of wild orange silk descended on her, wielding a dagger and giving out a high-pitched scream as it stabbed at the air. Hettie threw off her assailant and Tilly and Irene Peggledrip responded by piling in on top of the creature, knocking the dagger out of its paw and across the floor. There was an almighty struggle as the catfight continued back down the hallway, adding to the carnage already visible on Bugs Anderton's carpets; the understated beige had become a sea of red and the random bloody paw prints on the wallpaper could, under different circumstances, have been a Turner prizewinner from the paw of Tracy Ermine.

The creature was finally brought down on the front lawn and lay exhausted in a heap of orange silk. Delirium was nursing a bloody nose, Irene Peggledrip's hat was floating in Bugs Anderton's ornamental pond, and Tilly's best purple cardigan was in shreds. Hettie was the only one still standing, but even she was feeling the effects of friendly fire as Delirium had elbowed her in the face twice during the scrum.

Bruiser appeared on the lawn. Taking in the situation, he crossed over to the seemingly passive cause of all the destruction. He bent down to lift the orange silk away from the creature's face as it lunged at him like a coiled spring. He sidestepped his attacker and it fled out of the gate and down the path which led to the back door of the Dosh Stores. Bruiser and the company of walking wounded gave chase in time to see Pakora Dosh leap into the now bubbling cauldron of her famous lamb and tomato curry. Her screams were over quickly and, within seconds, the curry had swallowed her, leaving no trace except the tiniest corner of orange silk which stubbornly floated on top.

The five cats stared in silence and the cauldron bubbled contentedly on the stove, as if nothing had occurred. It was Irene Peggledrip who eventually broke the silence. 'Well, there's one for the freezer, that's for sure.'

Hettie was warming to Irene and her strange concept of the afterlife. The idea of a giant freezer containing the souls of murderers locked in ice appealed to her, and although the theory was uncertain, there was no doubt that curries would be off the menu for some time to come. She switched off the gas under the cauldron, leaving Pakora to stew in her own juice, and took in her surroundings for the first time. The kitchen was large and obviously doubled as a dayroom where Pakora spent her time. Its walls were adorned with exotic accoutrements – silk pictures of faraway temples, a collection of ivory tusks and a set of daggers with jewels that shone from the ornately carved handles. There were, of course, two missing.

'Come on,' said Hettie, rallying her bedraggled army. 'There's cleaning up to do next door and someone needs to get in touch with Lavinia Spitforce. She's in for a bit of a shock when she gets home.'

The shock had already descended. Lavinia had just arrived home and stood shaking in the doorway of Bugs Anderton's house as Hettie and co approached down the garden path. She looked small and vulnerable, not at all the haughty harridan that Hettie had so recently shared a spat with. 'Miss Spitforce,' Hettie said. 'I'm so very sorry.'

Lavinia took in the assembled company and burst into tears. 'It's all my fault. I should have believed her – she said she didn't feel safe here any more and I laughed at her. She'd been getting these nasty letters, you see, then Pakora came to see her last night and I heard them arguing. Pakora said some really vile things to her because she wouldn't sell the house to her.'

Irene Peggledrip moved to comfort Lavinia as Hettie and Tilly pushed past them and made their way down the hall to start the clean-up.

'Miss Bagshot! You are so very welcome.'

Hettie froze as Tilly cannoned into her. 'It can't be another bloody ghost!'

The lurid vision of Bugs Anderton rose up before them in all her gory glory. 'Miss Bagshot – as you are here and I am still in the land of the living, I must owe you a great debt of gratitude. But I doubt that my carpets will recover. Curry is one of the most stubborn of stains.' With that, Bugs Anderton fainted clean away and Hettie and Tilly dragged her into her armchair, placing her in the recovery position before informing the rest of the ensemble that Bugs Anderton had unseasonably arisen from the dead.

Hettie's heroes – as they would be known in future conversations – scurried round doing their best to clean up the trail of lamb and tomato curry that had been understandably mistaken for blood. Lavinia sat with Bugs; Delirium was naturally on beverages, assisted by Bruiser and Tilly, who had discovered a tin of freshly baked shortbread; Irene Peggledrip set to with the scrubbing brush, giving the beige and cream carpets a blush pink effect which wasn't unattractive; and Hettie phoned Balti Dosh to inform her that her Aunt Pakora was simmering in a vat of curry. She'd hoped to speak with Rogan, but surprisingly he wasn't available.

When a relative peace had descended on the house, everyone assembled in Bugs's sitting room to drink tea and eat shortbread, knowing that there was a story to come. Bugs – curry-stained and slightly scratched after her ordeal – didn't disappoint. 'As some of you know, I'd had these unpleasant letters and odd things happening in my garden. I told Pakora and she was very sympathetic; in fact, she suggested that I sell my house to her and move into the town or even back to Scotland to get away from the problems. I didn't realise until last night that it was her. She came round and asked if I'd made up my mind to sell. I told her that I was happy here and was engaging Miss Bagshot to investigate the problems. She got very angry, and if Lavinia hadn't been in her room I think she might have attacked me there and then. She left and I spent a restless night wondering what to do next. I phoned

Miss Bagshot first thing.' Hettie fidgeted slightly as all eyes turned to her and then back to Bugs. 'I suppose I was a bit stupid, really, but I spent the morning considering Pakora's offer on the house, weighing up the pros and cons. I eventually decided to go round and tell her that my decision stood and I would not be selling up. We were in the shop, and suddenly she flew at me like a cat possessed, screeching and screaming. She took hold of me and dragged me through to her kitchen. I felt so helpless, and she tied me to one of the kitchen chairs and forced a potato into my mouth. I could hardly breathe, and the more I struggled the more she screamed at me. I gave up and tried to sit still, hoping she would calm down, and she did.'

Bugs had a captivated audience now. Even Bruiser was hanging on her every word and Tilly and Delirium both nibbled nervously on their shortbread. Lavinia reached across and held one of Bugs's paws as she continued with her harrowing account. 'Pakora pulled up a chair beside me. It was terrifying. I'll never forget that face so close to mine, but nothing could have prepared me for what she had to say. She told me that she always got what she wanted and was very happy to kill for it. She said she was very clever at organising little accidents for cats who wouldn't sell their houses and businesses to her. She told me that she was descended from the great Jalfrezi Dosh, who had wiped out the Myers family to extend his empire, only to be thwarted by Thaddeus, who survived the massacre. She said that Thaddeus had followed Jalfrezi to India to avenge his family and had killed him in a duel, winning from him a box of gold coins as blood money. She said she didn't make mistakes like that and would succeed where Jalfrezi had failed.'

Hettie was getting impatient. It was good to know that justice had been done and that the puzzle over the box of gold sovereigns had been explained, but as fascinating as the back story of Milky Myers was, she felt she had to move things on. 'Did she confess to killing Mavis Spitforce?' she asked.

'Oh yes. She said it was her master plan to get Bhaji involved with Lavinia so that they would inherit Mavis's house and Rogan's store could be extended. Mavis realised what was happening and tried to protect Lavinia by sending her to me and leaving her house elsewhere.' Irene glanced down at her ridiculous Persian slippers, Lavinia allowed a tear to trickle unchallenged down her face, and Bugs Anderton continued. 'She said that Mavis had been poking her nose into the past and had to suffer for it. She said she enjoyed killing her and dressing her up. She told me she'd choked her first by forcing her to eat some pages from Marmite Sprat's little book. I didn't really understand what she said next, but it was all about a fat girl squealing like a pig and being strung up as a warning to anyone who told tales.'

Hettie clarified the situation, explaining to those who didn't know that Pakora Dosh was obviously referring to the murder of Teezle Makepeace. Teezle, by discovering Mavis Spitforce's body, had set her own death in motion by helping Hettie with her initial enquiries. But there was a question regarding her death which Hettie felt sure Rogan Dosh would be able to answer; it hadn't escaped her notice that he may have killed Teezle under Pakora's instructions, as well as disposing of her body.

Bugs drained her tea. Encouraged by Lavinia, she carried on with her account. 'I think I could laugh about it now, but in the middle of telling me about her killing spree the shop door went and she actually went through to serve a customer, leaving me tied up. She came back five minutes later and said it was time for some fun. She excused herself to lift a huge cooking pot onto the stove, and I could see it was full of curry. Then she pulled one of her daggers off the wall and held it above my head. I really thought that was it, but she sliced through the rope she'd tied me up with and held the dagger to the back of my head. She told me to stand up and walk forward towards the kitchen range. Then she flew at me, lifting me off my feet and forcing my head into the cooking pot on the stove. She kept pushing my head into the curry as I fought for breath. The potato she had wedged in my mouth came free and I began to scream. There was curry everywhere and she slipped on it, loosening her grip on me. Finding the strength from somewhere, I literally ran for my life through the shop and back to my house. She caught up with me at the front door, forced her way into the hallway and started wielding her dagger at me. We were both screaming, then everything went black. When I managed to open my eyes, she was gone.'

Lavinia gave Bugs's paw a reassuring squeeze. 'I thought you were dead,' she said. 'You wouldn't wake up, and everywhere was such a mess. I thought it was blood.'

Hettie felt that it was time to leave Lavinia and Bugs to their own devices. Delirium and Bruiser collected up the tea things and stacked them in the kitchen, and after a genuine vote of thanks from Lavinia on behalf of Bugs, Hettie and her merry band said their farewells and were waved off, hoping to meet up at the Butters' bonfire party the following night. Irene Peggledrip decided to accept Delirium's kind offer of a lift home on her pink scooter and they set off at a sedate pace in the direction of the town, narrowly missing a Dosh Stores van which appeared to be driven by a maniac.

The van screeched to a halt outside the shop as Hettie and Tilly were clambering wearily into their sidecar. Bruiser stiffened, ready for trouble, but it was Bhaji Dosh who emerged. Leaping over the gate that Tilly had just shut behind her, Bhaji ran the full length of the concrete path into Lavinia's arms. 'I'd say that may well be a happy ending,' Hettie predicted, settling down and pulling the rug up to her chin. 'Home for supper, Bruiser, and a pipe or two of catnip.'

Tilly giggled. 'I just thought of a joke.'

'Go on then, let's have it.'

'Well, I suppose you could say that Pakora Dosh has just committed Hurry Curry!' The friends laughed all the way home.

CHAPTER THIRTEEN

November 5th dawned bright and frosty. Tilly had been up for some time, working off the excitement and anticipation of the Butters' bonfire party; she'd put fresh batteries in her torch and counted the extra-long matches several times to make sure that there were enough for Hettie's firework display that evening. Bruiser had popped in for an early morning cup of tea, filling the coal scuttle in return, and he was now indulging in a tremendous amount of banging and hammering in the back garden, under the careful instruction of Beryl Butter.

Exhausted from her investigations, Hettie had

slumped in her chair the night before, inhaled a pie for supper and fallen into a deep sleep, allowing the world to move happily on without her. Only now, as Tilly divided a cheese triangle between two slices of toast, did she make any attempt to open her eyes. Sensing a slight movement from the armchair, Tilly seized the moment and put two more slices of bread in the toaster, then prepared Hettie's mug for her morning tea – even though the clock on the staff sideboard was heading rapidly for midday.

The final nail in the coffin of Hettie's lie-in came when the telephone burst into life. Tilly abandoned the toaster and scrambled into the sideboard, snatching the receiver from its hook. 'Hello? Tilly speaking. Oh, Miss Spitforce – how can we help? A meeting? Yes, I think we could manage that. Two o'clock at Whisker Terrace. Thank you. Goodbye.'

'What was all that about?' asked Hettie, as Tilly backed out of the sideboard. 'Not more trouble, I hope.'

'I'm not sure if it's trouble,' Tilly said, returning to the toaster. 'That was Lavinia Spitforce. She's having a meeting round at Mavis's house, and she wants us to be there.'

'Probably selling off the fixtures and fittings,' Hettie mumbled, struggling into an upright position to receive her tea and toast. 'And whatever is going on in the Butters' garden? What's all that banging?'

'It's Bruiser. He's doing a little job for Beryl.'

'Well it's a bloody noisy little job, that's for sure. And at this time of day, when any cat with an ounce of self-respect would be fast asleep.'

Tilly chose not to point out that it was now after midday. Sensing that one of Hettie's rants was about to gain momentum, she placed two rounds of cheese triangle on toast on Hettie's armchair and retreated to a safe distance to choose a suitable assortment of clothes from the filing cabinet for their meeting.

They decided to walk to Whisker Terrace, as Bruiser was obviously not available to take them in Scarlet: he seemed to be fighting some sort of battle at the bottom of the garden with the assorted planks of wood that had been delivered by Prunes and Pots. The bonfire for the party stood tall and proud in the November sky, and a pale, wintry sun brought the garden to life as the night's frost sparkled and melted away. Tilly could hardly contain her excitement, and even Hettie was looking forward to her role as artistic director of fireworks. 'We can't be long at Whisker Terrace,' she said, as they strode off down the High Street in their business macs. 'There's a lot of planning still to do for tonight. We need to get the bottles in place for the Rockets and the Catherine Wheels nailed to the fence before anyone turns up.'

'Then there's the toffee,' said Tilly, clapping her paws together. 'Betty says I can dip the apples for her.'

Hettie laughed at her friend's enthusiasm, wondering at the same time if the combination of Tilly and toffee was destined to come to a sticky end.

Thoughts of the bonfire party were quickly eradicated from their minds as they rounded the corner into Whisker Terrace. The Dosh Store was closed and they were met by a stream of parked vehicles: Irene Peggledrip's Austin Seven; the Dosh Store's van, thrown half-on, half-off the pavement; and Delirium Treemints's pink scooter, which seemed to have come to an ungainly halt on the path leading to the late Mavis Spitforce's front door. Bugs Anderton's cream Morris convertible was newly arrived and was shunting up and down, tucking itself in as close to the pavement as possible in front of the Austin.

Hettie was beginning to wonder whether the Friendship Club had found a new venue when Bugs Anderton fell out of her driver's seat wearing a rather risqué bright red winter cape. 'Oh Miss Bagshot! Welcome indeed to you and Miss Tilly. I'm so pleased you could join our little gathering.' Bugs lurched round to the passenger side of her car and hauled Mildred Spitforce out onto the pavement, looking resplendent in a caramel fun-fur and mock suede cowboy boots.

'I'm beginning to feel slightly underdressed,' said Hettie, following Bugs and Mildred round to the back of the house and into the kitchen, where the rest of the company was assembled.

The prime positions round the table had already been taken by Irene Peggledrip, Balti Dosh and Lavinia, but Lavinia offered her seat to Mildred, who gratefully settled herself down and kicked off the cowboy boots which had clearly been pinching since she bought them. Delirium had stationed herself by the kettle and was now taking orders for beverages, and Bhaji stood behind his mother, beaming a handsome, boyish grin at anyone who looked in his direction. Hettie and Tilly settled themselves against the kitchen cabinet by the door, hoping for a quick exit, and Tilly smiled with satisfaction as she looked at the assembled company: it was just like the final chapter from one of Miss Agatha Crispy's novels, where all the loose threads were tied up and the leading characters melted away into obscurity. Hettie, on the other hand, was wondering why she had had to give up more of her time when the weight of chief firework officer was bearing down on her and there had been no visible signs of lunch. A cat couldn't exist on cheese triangles alone.

It was Lavinia Spitforce who called the meeting to order. 'Friends – and I think after what we have all been through I can call you that – I have brought you together today because a number of decisions have been made which will go a long way to making life better for us all. I am aware of the trust my late aunt put in Miss Hettie Bagshot and her detective agency, and I thought it only right to include her today in the hope that we should gain her approval of the plans we wish to put into motion. In fact, without the help of those at the No. 2 Feline Detective Agency, at least one of us wouldn't be here today.' Hettie and Tilly fidgeted as all eyes turned to them, then, as one, swung in the other direction to where Bugs Anderton was picking threads out of the late Mavis Spitforce's tea towels. 'For my own part,' Lavinia continued, 'there are those I have hurt out of anger, but I understand now that you were all just looking out for me.' Bhaji gave an extra special beaming smile around the kitchen and squeezed Lavinia's paw. 'There is much healing to do,' she said, wiping a tear away, 'and Bhaji and I have decided to go to India. He wishes to explore his music, and I am looking for an inner peace which I know I will find with him. I am, however, aware that he must assume responsibility for his family and their business in the absence of his father, who has run away in shame at his association with Pakora and her terrible crimes. It is family that will save the day, and we have spoken this morning of a plan which will allow Bhaji his freedom and bring our families closer together.'

By now, Hettie was hoping for a decent punchline or at least a tray of Balti's samosas, but it was not to be. Sensing her distress, Tilly grubbed around in her mac pocket and produced a catnip biscuit covered in fluff, which Hettie received gratefully and sucked on quietly while Lavinia revealed her master plan. 'We have spoken with Balti, and she is happy to continue to run the Dosh Stores here in the town with some part-time help, which leaves the business out at Much-Purring-on-the-Rug. Bhaji and I were hoping to keep it in the family, and we wondered if my mother Mildred might be interested in running it for us while we're away on our travels?'

All eyes turned to Mildred, who had threatened to nod off but was now sitting up straight, suddenly the centre of attention. 'Me! Running a shop! In a little village in the country!' she exclaimed. 'You're 'avin' me on! No one gives me a chance like that. What would I know about shops? I've never had the money to spend any time in 'em.'

The company laughed nervously, and Balti came to the rescue, patting Mildred's paw reassuringly. 'No worries there, Mildred. We shall close the village shop for a couple of weeks while Bhaji and Lavinia decorate your new home, and you can come and learn the trade from me while you're waiting to move in.'

Mildred looked even more confused. 'New home! Where? And what about me flat and all me things?'

It was Bugs Anderton's turn to take centre stage, and she rose to the challenge in style. 'I have decided to sell my house after all and move back into the town. After what happened, I've no wish to remain in a place with bad memories and I have agreed to sell to Lavinia and Bhaji, who wish to make it their family home. I'm delighted to say that includes you, Mildred.'

Lavinia, seeing the look of shock on Mildred's face, added her own words of reassurance. 'Only if you want to, of course. If you'd rather stay in your flat, that's fine. We could get a manager in for the shop while we're away, but we wanted it to stay in our family and you can have your own space at the house to do what you like. We'd love to have you there.'

All eyes turned once again to Mildred, and even Hettie held her breath. Before she could respond, Irene Peggledrip rose from her kitchen chair and began to make a deep-throated gurgling sound, culminating in a puffing out of her cheeks. Bugs Anderton reached into the sink for the washing up bowl, convinced that Irene was going to be sick, but suddenly – as if she were in the room – the voice of Mavis Spitforce came clearly from the medium's mouth. 'Mildred, my dear sister, take your happiness while it is offered, mend what I have broken, live a long and happy life.' With that, the voice stopped and Irene Peggledrip lapsed into a bout of violent hiccups which were eventually brought under control by a slap across the face from Delirium Treemints.

Irene Peggledrip looked as bewildered as the rest of the gathering as she came to her senses, but Mildred Spitforce seemed to glow with a new understanding. 'If I'm to be family, I must share my fortune with you,' she said, turning to Lavinia. 'Thaddeus Myers's legacy has been passed down the family and now his sovereigns rest with me. I'll give them to you and Bhaji as my contribution to our future.'

A cheer went up around the kitchen as Bhaji produced a bottle of Dosh Stores fizz from behind his back. With the party now in full swing, Hettie and Tilly said their farewells with much patting of backs and made their way home, satisfied that the Milky Myers case had finally been solved and that the No. 2 Feline Detective Agency had notched up another triumph. Hettie's only hope now was that the firework display would go the same way.

CHAPTER FOURTEEN

Betty and Beryl Butter's garden was a hive of activity by the time Hettie and Tilly arrived home. The bakery had shut early to allow for the frantic preparations for the bonfire supper, and both bread ovens had gone into overdrive with the sheer volume of pies, pastries and fancy biscuits. Falling over the threshold, half-dead with hunger, Hettie was happy to help Beryl by devouring two beef pasties which weren't 'quite perfect', having met with a slight accident during their retrieval from the oven. Tilly was also keen to oblige, and chewed her way through some slightly damaged parkin biscuits.

Brushing the crumbs from their macs, they changed

into thick, warm jumpers and wellington boots and headed out into the garden to see what was to be done. Bruiser clearly hadn't stopped all day, and was now helping Betty to lay out two long trestle tables ready to receive the food. To one side was a bubbling cauldron of hot sticky toffee, mounted on a Calor gas ring.

'Perfect timing, Miss Tilly,' said Betty, leading her towards a mountain of apples on sticks. 'Get stuck in with these. Toffee's just right fer dippin'.' To demonstrate, she took up an apple by its stick and plunged it into the boiling toffee, spinning it once before bringing it safely to land stick-up on a metal tray. Needless to say, the toffee apple was perfect, a work of art, and by the time Tilly had finished it would still be the only perfect one – but nobody would mind once the bonfire party had begun. The main problem would be how quickly Tilly could pick and chew all the dried dollops of toffee off her jumper over the coming weeks.

Hettie joined Bruiser in setting up the folding chairs, conscious that the light was beginning to fade and the Catherine Wheels needed to be nailed to the fence while she could still see what she was doing. There was, however, one of the most difficult tasks still to come. 'We gotta get that knitted Guy on top o' that bonfire somehow,' Bruiser pointed out, 'and the sooner the better before it gets dark.' Hettie nodded in agreement and they strode purposefully back to the yard, where Mr Fawkes loomed over the coal bunker as if he'd already started on the bonfire punch. Taking one-leg each, they dragged him down the garden path, inadvertently uprooting a number of Brussels sprout plants along the way. The bonfire stood tall and magnificent against the darkening sky. Bruiser had done a fine job of laying and stacking cardboard, wood and old newspapers, ready for the crowning glory, although it would have helped if Lavender Stamp had run out of wool before this year's offering reached quite such gigantic proportions.

'I think it's a case of pushin' and shovin',' said Bruiser, opening a pair of tall stepladders and placing them next to the bonfire. 'I'll get onto the top step and you shove Mr Fawkes up after me. I got some string in me pocket so I'm gonna try and get him tied to the bit o' wood that's stickin' out the top.' It all sounded a bit technical to Hettie, but she understood her role, at least, and positioned herself between Mr Fawkes's legs, lifting him slowly up the stepladder towards Bruiser. All might have gone well had it not been for a pie landslide that took their attention at the crucial moment. Back up the garden, one of the trestle tables buckled suddenly under the weight of Beryl's pork lattice. Beryl acted quickly, shoring up the end of the table as her sister formed a makeshift safety net with her apron, successfully preventing the lattice delights from hitting the deck. Miraculously, only one pie was deemed un-servable and that was soon shared amongst the workers.

In truth, Hettie was simply no good with heights, and after the first abortive attempt to get Mr Fawkes up the ladder she was more than thrilled to see her old friend Poppa striding down the garden, munching on a slice of lattice pie. 'Wotcha!' he said, helping Hettie out from under the weight of the super knit. 'I think you'd better leave this to us. This is boys' work.' Hettie had always used her feminine wiles to escape the more tedious aspects of life, so she gladly gave up Lavender Stamp's effigy into the paws of her heroes and retreated to her shed in search of a hammer, nails and a large collection of empty milk bottles. So intent was she on her mission that she hadn't even noticed the new addition to the bottom of the Butters' garden . . .

She enlisted the help of Betty's wheelbarrow to transport the bottles to what she liked to call her display site, halfway up the garden and away from any trees or buildings. The clear run of fencing was perfect for the Catherine Wheels, and Hettie lined up the empty milk bottles at intervals along the bottom, ready to receive the rockets. Satisfied that all was in place, she made her way back up the garden to collect the fireworks, hoping that Tilly would be available to assist, but she was nowhere to be seen. The cauldron was redundant, the ladle cast aside, and the Calor gas ring turned off.

'If you're looking for Miss Tilly, she's in the sink,' said Betty, bustling out of the back door with an industrial-sized tray of parkin biscuits. 'I think the toffee got the better of her, so Beryl put her in to soak for a bit. She's made a good job of them apples, though – they've covered a treat, just like her really.' Hettie left Betty chuckling as she went in search of her firework assistant.

Tilly's warm jumper lay abandoned on the floor of their room and the sink area was a solid wall of bubbles, wobbling like an out of control jelly. To make the vision even more surreal, it was huffing, puffing and uttering the occasional expletive. Hettie approached with caution. 'Are you in there?'

The bubbles parted as Tilly sneezed a hole in them. 'It's not too bad now. I've managed to separate my paws, but one of my ears has folded over and stuck to my head and my whiskers are still solid with the stuff.' Hettie did her best not to make matters worse by laughing; Tilly was clearly putting on a brave and optimistic face, even if it was a little sticky. 'Let's have a look at you,' she said, teasing the toffee away from the offending ear which suddenly popped back into place. 'Not sure what to do about those whiskers. I think you'll have to put your head under to loosen them up.'

Tilly knew that Hettie was right, but it was a remedy she had been avoiding: any cat would prefer to keep her head above water in times of stress, but there was nothing for it if the whiskers were to be returned to their former glory. Taking a very deep breath, she slid under the bubbles, securing herself against the side of the sink with her newly released paws. Seconds later, she emerged spluttering and shaking her head. Hettie – pleased, that she was still wearing her wellingtons – teased the whiskers and successfully removed several strands of toffee. 'One more dip should do it,' she said, trying to remain positive. In fact, it took another fifteen minutes of underwater exploration before Tilly was able to sit on her blanket by their fire, toffee-free and wrapped in a bath towel.

The knock-on effect of the toffee incident was that Hettie was even further behind with her display preparations, and the arrival of Lavender Stamp in the backyard – ready to take up her annual position at the entrance table – panicked her. She pulled out the fireworks from under their table and began to decant them into a large empty crisp tin that Beryl had supplied, picking out the Catherine Wheels to nail to the fence. Tilly, catching the faint smell of gunpowder, struggled out of her towel and plumbed the depths of the filing cabinet once again, hoping to find something warm enough to wear. 'That's one best cardie and a good warm jumper ruined in just two days,' she grumbled as she finally settled upon a bright orange knit with a hood.

'Well, you'll just have to spend a day with Jessie next week choosing some new winter stuff from her shop,' said Hettie. 'We're in funds at the moment thanks to Mavis Spitforce, and your best cardie *was* ruined in the line of duty.'

Tilly's unstuck toes curled with delight at the thought of a shopping spree in her friend's charity shop, and as if by magic, Jessie popped her head round the door. 'Anything I can do to help?' she offered, looking magnificent in a red double-breasted maxi-coat with pink wellingtons and a moon-and-star-decorated cloche hat of midnight blue. 'I brought you the evening paper. No. 2 FDA all over the front page again. Nice one!'

Hettie took the newspaper and smiled with satisfaction as she read the headline: STRANGE BUT LIES. MILKY MYERS INNOCENT. She scanned the story briefly, noting that it was continued on pages three and four, and left it to Tilly and Jessie to paw over the finer points of an interview given by Balti Dosh, who wasted no time in singing the praises of them all.

It was growing dark by the time she reached her display site. Under Betty's instruction, Bruiser and Poppa were lighting hurricane lamps around the garden and hanging them from the trees. It was bitterly cold, but mercifully the wind had stayed away. Looking to her right, Hettie could see that Lavender Stamp's contribution to the bonfire party was looking resplendent, perched on top of his funeral pyre. Taking

244

up her hammer and nails, she quickly banged the Catherine Wheels into place along the fence, ensuring that they would all be free to spin when the time came. She filled an old bucket with water from the outside tap, ready to deal with any unwanted hazards, and swept clean the concrete slabs that she had chosen for her ground displays. Feeling like the hangman who had successfully calculated the drop, Hettie blew her paws against the cold and turned to make her way back up a garden now bathed in lantern light.

But she was thwarted in her bid for ten minutes at her own fireside by Betty Butter, who sailed down the garden path with a tray of hot chocolate, followed by her sister Beryl and a happy band of helpers which now included Tilly and Jessie. 'Gather round, all of you! My sister and me's got a little presentation to make before the party starts. Get yerselves a mug of chocolate and follow me.'

Betty led the company to the bottom of the garden, where Poppa and Bruiser were putting up the last of the lanterns. The soft light now illuminated a new wooden structure, in close proximity to Hettie's shed. It was an odd sort of building – a long, thin shed with a stable door and a lean-too roof, and Hettie remembered seeing something similar at one of the festivals she'd played at in a farmyard in Somerset. That one had stored a tractor. So this was the little job which had kept Bruiser busy earlier in the day.

'Now some of you will know,' Betty began, 'that we have a new lad in the yard, so to speak. Mr Bruiser Venutius has made himself invaluable of late with some of the jobs my sister and I have no likin' for these days. He has also joined the No. 2 Feline Detective Agency as chief driver and protector, so my sister and me decided to solve a couple of problems by 'avin this nice bit of shed put up. Firstly, some of our neighbours have taken against the parkin' up of a certain bright red motorbike and sidecar.' With this, Betty shared a knowing nod with Lavender Stamp and Hettie shrank back into her warm jumper, hoping it would make her invisible. 'Now Scarlet, as she is called, can rest herself in her new purpose-built shelter away from parkin' difficulties. Furthermore, Bruiser will always have a shed to rest his bones in on a winter's night – or any other night, for that matter. He now has an official address and a permanent home to return to, as and when.'

Hettie marvelled at the clever and diplomatic way in which Betty had handed over the little shed to a cat who had lived under the stars and by his wits for nearly all his life. Bruiser was no longer young, but he would never have admitted to the vulnerability that faced all cats whose days of travelling the highways and byways were over, and the Butters had saved his pride beautifully. A cheer went up and the hot chocolate mugs clinked a toast into the bonfire night sky as Bruiser – stunned by the Butters' generosity – sported a grin from ear to ear. With one swift bound, he engaged both the Butter sisters in a circular dance of sheer joy, leaving them catching their breath as he opened his stable door to inspect his new home.

Lavender Stamp was the first to peel away from the jolly company, sensing that the hour had come to position herself at the entrance table ready for the first guests to arrive. The Butters took up their stations behind trestle tables laden with every pie and pastry a cat could dream of, and Jessie manned the punch bowl, filling small cups with her special treacle, lime and orange cordial – a recipe that Miss Lambert had entrusted to her in her will.

Hettie and Tilly returned to their room for a final strategy meeting over the fireworks and the order in which they should be lit. Tilly collected the packets of sparklers to distribute among the guests she particularly liked, making sure that she had plenty for herself, and the two cats returned to the garden to find the bonfire supper in full swing. The Butters' guest list included most of their fellow traders in the High Street – Elsie Haddock, Hilda Dabit, Mr Malkin and Mr Sprinkle and their families, Lotus Ping from their haberdashery department, Doris Lean from the food hall, and her sister, Clippy, who had just won the Bus Conductress of the Year Award. Mr Prune and Mr Pots were enjoying a break from their garden centre, and Turner Page was enthralling the single female cats with the delights of his soon-to-be-opened new library. Meridian Hambone had arrived in her motorised wheel chair, customised by her mechanically minded son. Lazarus had dragged his plaster cast the length of the High Street, reluctant to miss an evening of pies and pastries, washed down by a glass or two of the home-brewed fiery ginger beer that Meridian had balanced on her knees in a plastic bucket all the way from their hardware shop.

There were pops, bangs and the occasional pretty shower of fireworks around the town, but there was no doubt that all eyes would be turned towards the bakery in the High Street for the main event, now the highlight of the November 5th celebrations. Hettie was understandably nervous, but she tried to calm herself by seeing how many different flavoured pies she could consume before eight o'clock, the agreed hour for her display to begin. Tilly was keeping a tally of pies consumed, and had only managed half of Hettie's input by the time they made their way back to their room to collect the fireworks, matches and torch.

Hettie pushed through the excited crowd with her tin box, followed by Tilly, and Jessie completed the small party, having been entrusted with the rockets. Poppa and Bruiser greeted them at the display site and acted as self-appointed safety wardens, keeping the crowd back to allow Hettie the space she needed.

Hacky Redtop pushed to the front with his notepad, dragging Prunella Snap and her camera with him. They were determined to bag the front page of the *Sunday Snout,* combining a 'case solved' angle with a triumphant pictorial display. Prunella was keen to get the ultimate shots, especially as she'd rather messed up the year before by absent-mindedly opening her camera and fogging the film before it reached her darkroom. It was a sad fact that Prunella's life – along with her photos – had always been a little over-exposed.

In a dramatic departure from tradition, Hettie decided to light the Catherine Wheels first. Taking the box of matches proffered by Tilly, she struck the first one and shot down the fence, lighting the blue tails until they all fizzled; retracing her steps, she set them all spinning with one startling paw movement and stood back as they burst into life, spilling their magical sprays of colour into the air and coming to an end at exactly the same time. The crowd responded with delight and wide-eyed anticipation of her next move. She nodded to Jessie, who brought forward stage one of Hettie's planned assault on the sky: four small rockets were placed in milk bottles, and once again Tilly stepped forward with the matches as Prunella Snap raised her Olympus Trip skyward. Working in reverse, Hettie lit the furthest touch paper first, moving backwards down the line until all four rockets sizzled ready for take-off. Then they were gone, like little red dragonflies up into the night sky. The party was silent as everyone tracked the tell-tale lights across the heavens. Hettie held her breath, knowing that her reputation rode on what happened next; for a moment, she doubted, and then came the triumph as the rockets exploded into showery fingers of every imaginable colour. The crowd whooped and cheered, Tilly cried with joy, and Hettie headed for the crisp tin to begin her ground displays.

Surprisingly, only one Golden Rain disappointed by fizzling out with a thud. It was immediately dispatched to Hettie's safety bucket, and the display continued to much applause until the tin box was empty. The grand finale involved Hettie, Jessie, Poppa and Bruiser all stationed in front of two rockets each, with Tilly moving swiftly down the line with the matches. At Hettie's signal, the rockets were ignited in perfect synchronicity and whooshed into the sky as one. The crowd began to count, and the sky exploded as the rockets danced and twisted in glittering showers of red, gold, silver and blue; eventually, they began to fall to earth, leaving a shimmering purple trail of dust which illuminated the joyful faces of all the Butters' guests.

A roar of approval went up as Hettie and her firework crew took their bows. Beryl signalled that sweet pastries and biscuits were now being served, and Bruiser and Poppa headed for the bonfire in preparation for the next stage of the party. Jessie returned to her punchbowl, which had been heavily laced by Meridian Hambone while no one was looking, and Hettie and Tilly – flushed with success – mingled and munched their way through a considerable quantity of bonfire treats.

The night had grown bitterly cold, and an air frost began to settle as the party dragged chairs and blankets to the bottom of the garden, ready for the lighting of the bonfire. Tilly, Hettie and Jessie perched on upturned flower pots right at the front, as Bruiser and Poppa put a match to each side of the giant pyre. Within seconds, the fire took hold and the flames began their journey towards Lavender Stamp's Mr Fawkes.

Hettie stared up at his face and suddenly all was quiet. The clapping and dancing had stopped, and snowflakes began to tumble from the sky. She rubbed her eyes, realising how very tired she was. The flames from the bonfire had turned blue and were giving out a strange, ethereal light. She shivered as the effigy began to disintegrate and the layers of wool peeled away, revealing a face she had come to know well. Jacob Surplus stared down from a throne of electric blue fire, and it was the most beautiful thing that Hettie had ever seen. He smiled, and his eyes bore into her, filling her with peace, then a host of figures began to form around him. Hettie knew that she was looking at the Myers family, then came Mavis Spitforce, and finally Teezle Makepeace. They all smiled down at her, and an important understanding passed between them.

'Are you all right?' asked Tilly, passing Hettie another shard of bonfire toffee as she twirled her own name with a sparkler.

'Yes,' replied Hettie with a smile, wedging the toffee into her mouth. 'I'm absolutely fine.'

To discover more great books and to
place an order visit our website at
allisonandbusby.com

Don't forget to sign up to our free newsletter at
allisonandbusby.com/newsletter
for latest releases, events and exclusive offers

Allison & Busby Books
@AllisonandBusby

You can also call us on
020 7580 1080
for orders, queries
and reading recommendations